W9-ADV-471

THE FORTUNES OF BRAK

John Jakes

A DELL BOOK

Published by
Dell Publishing Co., Inc.
1 Dag Hammarskjold Plaza
New York, New York 10017

ISBN: 0-440-12787-4

Printed in the United States of America
First printing—January 1980

CONTENTS

DEVILS IN THE WALLS

Lordlings, here the treasure lies,
Guarded round by rats and daws,
Maggots, worms, and cats who come
Creeping on a thousand claws.

Lordlings, in your greed and haste,
Hear a word to give you pause.
Will you face the cats who prowl
Slaying with a thousand claws?

Lordlings, if your lust remains,
Think upon their hungry maws—
Enter, and 'twill be your blood
Shining on my thousand claws.

—*Hamur's Enchantments*

"What am I bid?" cried the auctioneer of the slave market. "What am I bid for this yellow-haired barbarian fresh caught on the trail that leads down from Samerind?"

Before anyone in the crowd could so much as utter the first syllable of an offer, Brak moved.

He formed a loop out of the chain that held him fast to the stone pillar. With a lunge he fastened the loop around the auctioneer's neck. There was a terrible fury in his big, scarred body; much of the rage was rage at himself.

He had been riding wearily through the cool morning a few leagues north of this accursed crossroads village when the slavers set upon him, mounted men with spears and nets. Right now the narrow-faced leader of the band, a sickly-eyed creature named Zaldeb, was out there among the gawkers.

The big barbarian was ill-prepared for an attack. He was still suffering the aftereffects of a feverish illness. He had lain for a month, unseeing, unhearing, on a couch in the house of the trader Hadrios in Samerind. Finally his powerful body fought free of the sickness, which had been brought on by wounds incurred escaping from the Logol Waste, after the Jewel City of the Quran fell, burning.

Old Hadrios and his daughter urged Brak not to depart on his journey until he was fully well. But the big barbarian was impatient to be moving again. Thus he lacked the strength and quickness of wit to fend off the howling slavers with the nets. Even so he'd taken the lives of four of Zaldeb's men before they broke his broadsword and slew his pony—

The auctioneer tore at the chain around his throat. His tongue popped out of his mouth. The big barbarian pulled the chain all the tighter, thinking, *And one more jackal dies before I do*—

The crowd shrieked and fell back. Tall, wide shouldered, naked save for the garment of lion's hide around his middle, the barbarian looked bestial as he toppled the auctioneer and fell on top of him.

Brak let go of the chain. He used his hands to choke the man's throat. But he wasn't destined to gain even this temporary revenge just then.

From behind a pillar rushed a crowd of the bullies who tended the town's now empty slave pens. They carried leather lashes and swung them with coarse yells of pleasure. One of the lashes snaked round Brak's head, a streak of fire across his eyes. He howled, tore at it.

Another lash ripped his back. Another. In a moment he'd been whipped into near-blindness and dragged away from his intended victim.

Bleeding, he was thrown against the stone pillar on the block. The auctioneer tottered to his feet. He rearranged his robes, massaged his throat. Then he walked over and delivered a vicious kick to Brak's middle. At the same time he blew spit in Brak's face.

The barbarian lurched forward on hands and knees. The auctioneer darted out of range. For a moment Brak remained on all fours, the long yellow braid of his hair hanging down over one shoulder, his eyes sullen with hate. Blood oozed from the lash marks all over his body.

He felt sick, humiliated. He reached for the auctioneer's leg. The crowd sighed in horror, then with relief.

Brak's chain was not quite long enough for him to catch his tormentor.

"See how he struggles!" the auctioneer exclaimed breathily. "A barbarian out of the wild lands of the north. He told the worthy Zaldeb that he was bound to seek his fortune in the warm climes of Khurdisan far southward. For a small price one of you out there can employ him to improve your own fortune. He has the strength of six men! He can till a field or turn a mill wheel all day and all night without falling. Keep him securely chained and you'll be perfectly safe, the owner of a splendid slave! Now what am I bid?" He clapped his hands. "Who will make the first generous offer for this valuable prize?"

"Ten dinshas," piped an elderly man.

"What's that? Ten?" The auctioneer sneered. "Yea, graybeard. I know hard times have fallen on the village of Yarah the Bull. Crops fail. Bellies gurgle in hunger. But can your purse be so thin that you would pass an opportunity to have such a fine slave for your own? Think again. I'll not sell this one for such an insultingly low price."

"Twenty dinshas," came another bid.

"Pfaugh! Still too little. Come, good friends. Consider well the—"

"*Make way.*" This time the voice was feminine. "*I'll pay you two hundred.*"

"Two hundred—?" The auctioneer nearly choked. "Do I hear another bid?" He did not wait long enough to find out, clapping his hands and crying, "I declare the wild man of the north sold to Mirande, daughter of Splendid Hamur, Prince of a Thousand Claws."

The auctioneer kicked Brak's thigh, bent down, and

growled, "And it's fitting that a brute like you should fall into her clutches. If anyone can take the arrogance from you, it's that strange and greedy slut."

The warning penetrated Brak's dulled mind. He liked it little.

In a moment he found all but his wrist chains loosened. He was freed from the pillar. Surrounded by the bullies with their lashes ready, he was hustled down through the crowd past the preening Zaldeb, into the presence of his purchaser.

She was a well-formed, dark-haired woman. She did not look especially old, except for long streaks of gray that marred her dark hair. She was richly attired in veils and girdles sewn with gleaming pearls. Brak noticed that people in the crowd were murmuring about him. Treating him to looks of sorrow; of pity. He wondered why.

The woman did not look like such a harsh mistress. Her face was well proportioned and rather attractive. Her skin was smooth. It would be easy, he imagined, to play the cowed slave with her. Gull her into thinking he was tamed. Then escape. Yes—simple. Or so he thought as he gathered his wits.

Abruptly he thought otherwise. Mirande treated him to a peculiar, intense, dark-eyed scrutiny.

Her voice, quiet, troubled him: "I've purchased you at a dear price, barbarian. I've hoarded my small store of dinshas until the day when a man of strength would at last be offered in this provincial marketplace. That day has been a long time coming."

"My name is Brak," he grunted, "not barbarian."

"You come from the high steppes, don't you? The wild lands northward?"

"Aye, lady. But I've seen enough of you so-called civilized people in my travels to say this much. I'm as good as you and perhaps better, since I lack the refinement of mind necessary to practice slavery."

Rather than angering Mirande, the remark amused her. "Can you use a blade as well as you employ your tongue?"

"Ask of the jackal there," he said, shaking his wrist chains at Zaldeb, who cowered back.

Before Mirande could say more, the crowd stirred. A herald beating on a hip drum and riding on an ass announced the arrival of the ruler of this territory, Yarah the Bull.

Brak raised his head. Perhaps he'd find Yarah a man to whom he could appeal sensibly, though his journey thus far on the road to Khurdisan cast doubts. He'd found the populated kingdoms to be strangely perverse and savage places in which learning, culture, wealth seemed to heighten greed and irrationality, rather than lessen it.

The sight of the fat, richly clad nobleman on an emaciated gray horse wrecked his hopes. Once Yarah the Bull might have been a mighty warrior. Now he had fallen into sloth. On second glance his rich apparel was seen to be threadbare, wine-stained. There were huge purplish pouches beneath his eyes.

Resting his gauntlets on his considerable paunch, Yarah the Bull watched Brak warily. Behind him six footmen held lances, ready.

"Are you the lord who rules here?" Brak demanded.

Yarah frowned. "I am the governor, chosen by the folk. You have a snarling tongue, outlander. I don't care for it." He appraised Brak's breadth of shoulder. "I must say the tales I heard were true. You're the first specimen of size Zaldeb has procured in a long time. I rather regret I arrived so late. I could use a strong arm in my household." He belched, then smiled in a sour way. "I would have given you better treatment than you'll receive from her, I'll vow."

Mirande stiffened ever so slightly. She said nothing. Brak's palms began to crawl.

"Governor," he said, "I was unjustly set upon—"

Yarah the Bull waved. "No, no. Trouble me not with appeals for freedom. The taking of able-bodied men for sale as slaves is an old, and legal, custom in our small province. In fact," added the governor with some sadness, "Zaldeb is doubtless the only man among us turning a profit these days. We've fallen into hard times. Our crops are bad, our people go hungry." He cast a queer, oblique look at the woman with the gray-streaked hair. "Perhaps she'll find a way for you to change all that. Provided, of course, you live past the setting of the moon tonight."

"You forget yourself, governor," said Mirande in a soft voice. "You forget who I am."

"No." Yarah picked at a pouch of fat under one eye. " 'Tis the opposite. I remember all too well." So saying, he touched rusting spurs to his spindly mount. He clattered off across the square.

Mirande tugged Brak's wrist chains. Four eunuchs in white linen clouts fell in behind the big barbarian. He contemplated making a break for freedom. But each eunuch carried a dagger of considerable length. Their eyes were empty, obedient to the woman's will. He decided to wait, letting himself be led out of the square past the last of the crowd. He wondered again why he received so many curious, pitying stares.

As though he were condemned to death.

The woman seemed mild-mannered enough, though aristocratic. Surely she wanted nothing except a strong companion for her couch. He was willing to gull her that way if necessary, until the opportune moment for escape presented itself.

He learned nothing of Mirande's motives on the walk to her house at the edge of the shabby village. The house was small, built around a central court where only weeds grew. The furnishings were poor, the walls peeling. The floors were in a dismal state of repair. Altogether the place was clotted with shadows and sour smells and seemed no better than other dwellings in the obviously poverty-ridden town.

When Brak had settled himself grudgingly upon a scrap of carpet beside an oil lamp, Mirande dismissed the eunuchs who had brought in a plate of meat joints and a cracked ewer of wine.

"Are you hungry, Brak?"

"Indeed."

"Then eat. You have my permission."

"That's very humane of you, lady."

She colored at his insolence but stifled a retort. He picked up a hunk of meat. It had a slightly tainted smell. The wine in the ewer was oily, cheap.

He ate and drank anyway, famished. Presently he began to feel in better control of his wits.

Mirande sat with her fingers interlaced between her knees, speaking only after he'd been eating for a while: "Would you be interested in knowing why I paid so much for you?"

"Two hundred dinshas does seem a considerable sum to one who has none."

"It's nearly all I had left."

Brak helped himself to wine again despite the repulsive, oily reek. "If you wish to tell me, lady, do. I'm your property, am I not?"

"But you have no stomach for bondage."

"No," he agreed, swilling some wine. He wiped his

mouth with the back of a brawny arm. "I'd as soon strangle you as make talk."

"Try," she smiled, "and my eunuchs in the hall will be on you instantly with knives."

"I'm aware," he nodded. "Why do you think I sit here like this?"

That brought a bigger, more appreciative smile to her red-painted mouth. "As I noted in the square, you seem to have intelligence as well as brawn. Don't let the former get in the way of the latter, however. I bought you for your strength. That I might give you a certain task to perform, and when it's done—" Strange lights filled her dark eyes. "—unlock your chains and set you free."

"No doubt this task will take me but eighty and eight years."

"If you have the courage for it, the task will take but an hour or two."

Brak sat up stiffly, his sun-darkened face clenching into a scowl. "If you're making sport of me—"

Shaking her head, Mirande led him to a keyhole window. In the distance, at the top of a hill out past the edge of the village, stood a crumbling pile of stone. The hour was growing late. Although there was sunlight still falling from behind Mirande's house, the moon was up. The weird, jumbled lights of night and day made the wrecked walls on the hilltop glow with a faint slimy radiance.

"That rubble," she said, "was once the palace of my father. He was not the elected governor of this land. He was the hereditary lord. I could not take his place because only male issue may be heir to the throne. Thus leadership passed to that bag of slops, Yarah. In my father's time this province was much larger. It extended north nearly to Samerind and south for an equal distance. My father was a mighty lord. Perhaps you've heard his name. Prince Hamur? Hamur of a Thousand Claws?"

Brak shook his head. "An unusual name, though."

"He was called Thousand Claws because he kept a thousand hunting leopards in cages below the ground on which the palace stands. He's long dead now. He left a threefold legacy." Dark eyes glowing in that odd way again, she raised three fingers. Slowly she bent one down.

"There is a treasure in those ruins, outlander. The store of forty years of riding out to plunder the lands nearby, and the caravans unlucky enough to pass this way. He was a bandit, my father. His treasure lies there to this day, rich beyond belief. It's mine by right."

Uneasy, Brak asked, "And the second part of the legacy?"

"A few of the fierce leopards prowl up there. Not many. But a few. Killers."

Silence. The lamp guttered. The eunuchs whispered somewhere out of sight.

"The third?" asked Brak with a feeling that he was pronouncing his own sentence.

"There are demons haunting the palace walls."

Presently Brak replied with a grunt. "I'll doubt none of the three, lady. I have encountered phantoms and other unspeakable things in my travels, not to mention the madness of men. But why are you here and the treasure there if it's yours by birthright?" There was a quick, hard gleam in his eye then and a coldness deep in his belly. "Or is the reason for that also the reason I was bought?"

With a merry laugh she tried to pat his head. "Wise—" He pulled back, clashing his teeth together.

She stared at him awhile, as if deciding whether to be angry. Eventually she suppressed rage and explained:

"Years ago, when I was a child, my father attacked a certain rich caravan a few leagues to the westward. He took forty persons traveling in that caravan as prisoners, brought them home to his halls, and there slew them for diversion. But a certain wizard, an itinerant maker of spells and sorceries who happened to be the brother of the chief caravaneer, and accompanying him south on this particular journey, was one of the victims. He put a curse upon Prince Hamur. As the wizard was dying, he promised that the tormented souls of the forty victims would dwell forever in the great hall of the palace. Their blood still smears the walls, great red-brown patches of it. And somehow they live beneath—*within*—those awful stains. Their avenging spirits drove my mother mad, then my father. She drowned herself in the moat. He wandered on the battlements one night and, seeing some terrible vision, jumped screaming to his death. The curse drove my nurse and me from those walls. She is dead a long time too. Only I remain. The palace, deserted now, has crumbled to a sorry state. Tonight, as every night, the demons will be standing guard over the hoard none has managed to carry away. In the past a few thieves—some from the town, others from leagues away—have tried to bring forth the riches still heaped in the central hall. The result—"

Dread wrapped around them in the failing light. Brak grunted, "Speak plain."

"Terrible death."

At last he understood. "So I'm to try?"

She seized his wrist. "The thieves were a dull, witless pack! For a man of strength and cunning—a man born to the savagery of the steppes, the wild places—besting the guardians might be a task that could be accomplished! I have spent my days since I fled that place waiting for such a one." She looked deeply into him and smiled her eerie smile. "For you."

"Ah. A nice choice. Enter the palace or remain enslaved." Brak's eyes narrowed. "Answer me this question. What's to stop me from strangling you dead this minute?"

Now Mirande's smile was merry again. She clasped her hands together. "Just this. I knew when I heard you speak to swing-belly Yarah that you were a man of some honor. Unlettered, perhaps. Savage by temperament. But honorable. For all your barbaric looks, I read that in your eyes. It becomes my strongest chain. A pretty trap to fall into, isn't it, Brak?"

Savagely sinking his teeth into his lower lip, Brak turned away. Gods curse him, the woman was right. The truly wise and clever man would slay her instantly, then reckon with the eunuchs as best he could. He could not. He swung around, the wrist chains clanking.

"Say again, in exact words, what I must do."

"Bring forth Hamur's treasure," Mirande whispered. "Bring it forth and go free."

"When must I go?"

"As soon as possible. I've waited—"

"Not tonight," he interrupted. "If I'm to duel with beasts and monsters, I'll need a bit of rest. Tomorrow. Put out the lamp and leave me."

On the point of arguing, she finally nodded to agree. She fetched several small medicine pots and applied stinging unguents to draw the fire from the lash marks on his back. Then she stole out. The lamp burned down.

Brak tried to sleep. He couldn't. Ever and again he rose to steal back to the keyhole window and stare at the wrecked palace of Hamur on the hill. Its slimed, decayed walls gleamed in the moonlight. Great black birds—ravens?—croaked and flapped above one remaining turret. Finally he did manage to doze off for a time. But his sleep was thin and unsatisfying. He woke to find that a chill mist had closed on the world.

As the light increased, Mirande appeared at the chamber door. She used a tiny key to unlock the manacles on his wrist. The chains clanked to the floor. From a wrapping of scarlet cloth she produced a broadsword of gleaming iron, unsullied by rust. The hilt was set with many gems.

"This is the best weapon I can offer you, Brak. It was a mighty weapon in the hands of Hamur of a Thousand Claws."

A wicked weapon, he thought. He didn't say it. He swung the blade once, twice, three times in the air. "The balance and temper seem decent." With a wild, dreamy smile he laid the sword edge athwart her neck.

She didn't blink, though the pulse in her throat grew visibly faster. "What's to prevent my running now, lady?" he asked.

"My eunuchs. And Yarah and Zaldeb. You can run, yes. But you'll be pursued as a runaway slave and slain. Wouldn't you rather travel to Khurdisan without forever looking behind you?"

He swore deep in his belly, and lowered the broadsword.

"Very well," he said, "let's climb the hill. 'Tis a dark day, but I'd rather enter now than by night."

They proceeded to the rear gate of the house and there mounted a pair of mangy white donkeys.

Mirande led the way along a rocky path up the hillside. Brak noted that the rooftops of the village were crowded with citizens who had risen early to watch. He began to feel like a sacrificial beast.

The coming of wan, misty daylight had not lessened the forbidding aspect of Hamur's haunted palace. Obscene curls of the mist wound around the fallen towers and caved-in rooms. As they drew nearer, Brak could clearly see the trickles of foul water on the outer walls. Foul mold grew everywhere, shining. A nauseous stench drifted to his nostrils. Mirande covered her face with a bit of silk, using her other hand to apply a short braided quirt to beat her donkey's flank.

They had progressed about halfway up the hillside when Brak heard a clattering of hooves behind.

He swung round, massive hand dropping to the jeweled hilt of Harmur's broadsword. Their pursuer was a man of medium height, with a plain face. He wore a gray cowl and robe, of a style and cut Brak thought he had encountered before.

Sure enough, there was the girdle of beads at the man's waist. And the small stone cross of pitted gray stone, which Brak found forbidding. The arms of the cross were of equal length.

Breathing hard, the man reined in his shaggy pony.

"The Nameless God forgive you, Mirande," said the new arrival. "I only returned to the village at midnight. I was told what you planned."

The man raised his stone cross by holding the lower vertical arm. Instinctively Brak shied his donkey back.

"I beg you, Mirande," the man went on. "Control your greed. Don't force this helpless slave to his death."

"Helpless!" Brak shouted, "Nestorian or no, that's one word no man can call me and—"

"I meant no insult!" exclaimed the man, likewise

backing his mount off. Then he gave Brak a closer look. "I am called Friar Benedic. You know my order?"

That question, so innocently posed, brought a sour smile to the barbarian's mouth. It was to the north, in the Ice-marches, that he had first encountered these priests of the ecstatic goatherd, Nestoriamus, and their doctrine of the Nameless God. According to a holy man called Jerome, with whom Brak had shared a perilous adventure, two elemental godforces warred endlessly for dominion over all the lands of men: Yob-Haggoth the Dark One, and this priest's beneficent god, who had no name. Already in his travels Brak had faced the wrath of Yob-Haggoth, both directly and in the form of the Dark One's minister among men. Every step Brak took on his journey to the golden crescent of Khurdisan was accompanied by the knowledge that this minister, the awful Septegundus, might be waiting for him anywhere, to bar his path and claim revenge.

Of the existence of Yob-Haggoth Brak was grimly certain. Of the strength of the Nameless God he was less certain, although he had seen a few baffling evidences of the power of that curiously frightening stone cross. Yes, he had indeed met Nestorian friars before, including another known as Pol, whom he had left dead in a cell of the Jewel City of the Logol Waste, just before the city's destruction.

All this the barbarian preferred to hide, saying only, "I know."

"Don't spoil your lips arguing with the crazed fool," Mirande spat. She maneuvered her donkey between the Nestorian's pony and Brak's mount. "Begone, Benedic. Take your pious words and your pretty little legends somewhere else. The spirits you study are different from mine. Mine are real—the very ones infesting the walls of the house of a Thousand Claws. Those can be dealt with by a strong man—a man who knows there's a tangible reward to be won, instead of the childish and ephemeral rewards you promise." Tugging on her donkey's rein, she started off. "Brak! I order you to follow me and ignore the meddler."

Staring into Brak's eyes, as if to convince him of the sincerity of his intent, Friar Benedic said, "Whoever you may be, take heed of this. The creatures haunting the blood-soaked walls of Hamur are things of the pit. Foul essences born of a curse that springs from one of man's worst passions—revenge. If you know my order as you say, then you also know the power of this." He held up the cross. "Sword iron will be as a willow wand inside those walls. Take this instead—"

"I have no faith in that," said Brak, which was basically true.

"Take it anyway. It has proved its power to the faithless many times. In this configuration, this symbol of the Nameless One, there is divine strength to overcome—"

Screaming, Mirande raised her quirt and lashed Friar Benedic across the face.

The priest cried out. He reeled and tumbled from his saddle, sprawling on the rocky earth. Blood ran from a long, deep wound in his cheekbone. Yet he had strength to cry at her, "Every man in the village knows you're sending a blameless slave to die, just so that your greed can be appeased. The Nameless God sees such injustice! It will not go unpunish—"

Mirande gave Brak's bridle a furious tug. The rest of the Nestorian's cry was lost behind a rattle of hooves as the two animals bolted up the slope.

By the time Brak caught up with the woman, a veil

of rage had fallen across his mind. He shouted, "What sort of heartless—?"

In answer she spun around and laid the quirt across his neck. "*Silence*! By law you're my slave. Bound to obey, not question!" As he wiped blood from the thick-muscled skin of his throat, she kicked her mount to the crest of the slope.

There she climbed down. The mist curled and snaked over the ground. A raven shot up from behind a rubble pile, wheeling off and disappearing into the murk. The palace was gained by the rotting planks of an old drawbridge, which led to a wrecked portcullis. The stench blowing from within the ruins was fetid, dismal.

Brak dismounted. He peered over the lip of the long-empty moat. A pair of swollen rats went scurrying along the dry bottom. He noticed what seemed to be a man's body a little further on. The body was sprawled on thorns growing wild where once the water had flowed. The man's robes and headcloth were gaudy, not yet having fallen into decay. But where there should have been the flesh of a cheek, Brak saw only bare white bone.

"Oh," said Mirande, noticing Brak's gaze. "His name was Akronos. A beggar of the village. A thief. He was the last one who tried to enter the palace for the treasure."

"His robes are still bright," the barbarian mused. "Yet his skull's bare, as if—as if he's been down there for centuries." After a pause he asked, "When did he come here?"

"No more than four nights ago."

"*Four—?*" Brak's eyes were huge. "What became of his flesh? Did carrion—birds?"

"No, Brak. His robes are not torn, can't you see

that? There are devils in the walls—" Abruptly she pressed herself against the huge man. Her gray-streaked hair blew in the damp wind. Her mouth was very close, and for the first time he could tell that she had been drinking wine that morning. "The devils slew him, Brak. They may kill you. But if they don't—you've the courage and skill to bring out the treasure—you can remain with me instead of riding on." Her fingers worked at the heavy muscle in his upper arm. "You can stay here as a free man. I can reward you with the kind of delight that befits courage—" All at once she kissed him; her eyes grew enraged when he shoved her away.

"I've made one pact with the pit already," he growled. "I'll not enter another." And carrying the jeweled broadsword of Prince Hamur, he strode onto the drawbridge, not looking back.

He felt Mirande's eyes following him. He resisted the temptation to see how ugly her face had become.

He passed the rotted portcullis, entered a vast courtyard where the mist swirled thick. In the murk piles of human bone gleamed here and there.

During the first part of their ride up the hillside Mirande had given him careful and elaborate instructions for locating the great hall. Without difficulty he found the arched portal that had once been the chief entrance of the palace. Once inside, however, even the fetid air of the courtyard seemed an unappreciated blessing.

He passed through long corridors and lofty chambers where once-opulent hangings drooped from the walls in mold-slimed tatters. Rats chittered and scurried in the debris littering the mosaic floors. Long festoons of dust hung down, brushing his face as he passed. Suddenly a black shape flapped at him—

With a wild yell he brought the broadsword up, flashing, and cleaved hard. The thing dropped, sundered. He bent to examine the remains. He discovered with a shiver that he had killed some species of bat. The creature had an enlarged head and oversized, curving teeth.

Passing on, the big barbarian reached a vaulted room with a sunken pool in the center. Down in this pool lay another human skeleton with numerous holes in the skull and breastbone. Brak sucked in breath, glancing around uneasily. What manner of fiend could strip a corpse of flesh so completely or gnaw holes in solid bone? A sense of gathering evil overwhelmed him. He strode wide around the pool.

Ahead a flight of stairs loomed: a once-magnificent staircase, now fallen to ruin. At the summit, according to Mirande, should be the great hall of Prince Hamur.

Brak stopped again. His back prickled where his long yellow braid hung down. In the distance he heard the unmistakable scurry of sandaled feet.

He waited. The stealthy sound did not come again. Somewhere water dripped.

Brak stepped over a fallen statue at the base of the stairs. His mouth soured when he saw that the artifact was an obscene depiction of a man and a woman. He began to climb the staircase with the jeweled sword gripped firmly in his right hand.

He reached the top, spun around. He could have sworn that the sound of the unseen walker reached his ears again.

"Who's there?" he shouted. "Who's hiding?"

Hiding hiding hiding. The echo ran away through limitless rooms of the dead. *Hiding hiding hiding*—

Brak was facing toward the bottom of the staircase.

Behind him he heard a muffled stir
sound; a rustling not of mortal origin.
his hands began to crawl.

Suddenly a voice came ringing from far away:
barian? Do you hear me?"

"Who speaks?" he thundered back.

"Your dear comrade Zaldeb, who follows your every step."

"Stinking slaver! Where are you? Show your face so I can cut it apart."

There was a sickly laugh, far away. "Nay, outlander, I'm hid where you'll never find me. And I've brought my stout bow along. Under this rotting ruin six leopards of mighty Hamur still live. I've already loosed them from their pens. When they've torn you to pieces, I'll slay them from long range with my arrows. Then I'll take the treasure for myself."

"You're suddenly brave," Brak mocked. "Have you never had guts to come here before—"

"Mirande never looked with such lust on a man before—"

Now Brak's laugh was cruel. "And you covet her? And jealousy—?"

"I'll prove I'm a man this day!" cried the distant voice. "I'll make her look at me and not through me, like a woman staring at a wine bottle! When I present her with the treasure and one of your thigh bones gnawed through, she'll see that Zaldeb is a worthy lover for—"

A wild, spitting sound in the distance hid the rest. Brak gnawed his lip. Zaldeb, driven by his craving for the woman, had loosed the leopards; of that he was sure. Not far off, the beasts, probably long unfed, were ticktacking over the mosaics with their long claws, and breathing out soft growls.

word, hacked through
. The rotted stuff fell
e him.
er, with many entrances
in the walls, small circular
d light. Brak advanced cau-
he room, where a huge, heavy
rned.
Hi lver cup. It rolled and clanged. He glance or the first time, drew in a long, sharp breath.

Ornaments and artifacts of silver, gold, brass, bronze, ivory were strewn across the entire floor. Jewels green and violet and amber and red gave off dull lights. The loot of the Prince of a Thousand Claws had been spilled out recklessly by time from rotted collapsed trunks and bales. There was treasure in such profusion that its accumulated worth defied Brak's imagination. It was as if he walked on a carpet of riches.

Abruptly the dry rustling began anew. There was a long, piercing cry.

Brak lifted his eyes from the field of treasure and looked at the walls. He went rigid.

When he had first entered the hall, he had noticed great stained places on the wall, dark in color. He had assumed these to be the discolorations of time. Now these stains began to shimmer and glow with pale red light. A moaning began too, as though souls called out in torment. The hideous marks on the walls—*blood of Hamur's victims,* thought Brak suddenly—began to blur and shift, pulsing with the reddish glow.

The walls were *alive.*

A black mist congealed over each stained place, then

swirled outward. The cry of unseen voices became higher, keener, as though the invisible demons no longer lamented, but sang of their lust for his life.

The black mist spun and churned, the clouds of it growing larger. Those clouds congealed on every side of him and billowed thicker by the second. A tendril of one cloud reached out for him, inhumanly cold—

A cough, a breathing snarl behind—

He twisted. The first cadaverous leopard slunk up the staircase and crouched at the entrance to the chamber.

In a moment its five companions followed. They were all incredibly long, low-slung, deadly. Their ribs stood out beneath their skins. Their huge yellow eyes saw him. Yet the clouds pouring off the walls seemed to check them, drive them lower onto their bellies, set them to whining—

Another tendril of cloud curled near Brak's arm. Awful pain shot through him.

He jumped away from the cloud. His foot skidded on a pile of jeweled armlets, and he fell. He made a great clattering among the treasure.

The foremost leopard lunged, then pulled up short. The six animals kept snarling and spitting, drool dripping from their fangs. But the clouds from the walls held them, and the unearthly shrieking grew all the louder.

Brak knew death was very close.

In the dim recesses of his mind he knew that his only escape lay in blunting the power of the demoniac life that clouded from the walls. The clouds were *alive*—and boiling closer on every hand. He leaped again as a tendril curled at his leg.

He reckoned that he might be able to fight his way out of the hall across the carcasses of six slain leopards. But in the time it took him to slay the beasts, the demoniac effluvium would be upon him, wrapping him, choking him, killing him—

The clouds came down, closing. The wails of the damned victims grew deafening.

A sword against them?

Useless.

Crouching, growling with barbaric savagery, Brak turned cold inside. There was no way—

Then, as if in a dream, an image came to him:

Friar Benedic extending his little stone cross.

Brak licked his lips, laughed in a broken way. Times before, he had seen the symbol of the Nameless God work a strange power over dark things. With a shaking hand he lifted the broadsword, leaped out, ran screaming like a berserker at the nearest cloud.

The moment the billows closed, the unearthly moaning reached an unbelievable mind-hammering intensity. He knew suddenly that he had cast lots and lost. He could not drive himself forward to complete his task. The unseen, hateful spirits in the poison mist were sucking his strength with their rage; numbing him; turning him colder than the old earth—

With legs and arms and torso shaking with a pain that was near to ecstasy, he staggered another step. He yelled at the top of his lungs, wild, steppe-born yells, the cry of the warrior driven mad by the gods of the kill.

On he stumbled, driving himself while the hell-mists whipped and tugged. His brain blurred. His lungs burned. His head was ready to burst. Then, suddenly, he found himself against the chamber wall.

The wall was no longer solid but viscous. It moved

with the crawl and the stench of the dead. It was a wall spongy to the touch.

Both hands on the haft of the broadsword, he raised the weapon high and brought it arching down. The iron point hacked a long vertical cut in the inhuman, crawling surface.

As though he had struck simultaneously into the bowels of ten thousand human beings, the cry of agony intensified till his ears vibrated with unspeakable pain.

Then his mouth cracked into a ghastly smile. The blackish stuff had thinned a little. The flaccidity had gone out of the wall where the track of his sword had left a white gash through ancient bloodstains.

Every thew in his huge frame straining, he swung the broadsword over his shoulder and brought it around with all his might. The savage swing cut a horizontal mark that intersected his first cut a little more than midway up.

White as eternity, the cross of the Nameless God glared out of the wall before him.

Almost in defiance he screamed his berserker's scream at that mark, telling it in a long, ululating cry to show its power if power there was—

Then, panting, he began to tremble with terror.

Around the cross of Nestoriamus the black cloud was rolling back.

With another wild cry Brak turned and dashed along the wall, stopping only to cut another mark with two hacks of his blade.

In this manner he raced around the chamber, hacking crosses on the wall and driving the demon-cloud before him. At last the cloud boiled and fumed only at the chamber entrance, confined there.

The tormented crying took on a new quality, became a persecuted, angry whine. Suddenly the hell-cloud dropped. The six crouching leopards began to tear at one another, leap and rake each other's flanks.

The cloud enfolded them. Brak saw it as a ghastly vision: whatever vile spirits of revenge and hate dwelled in these walls were now striking the life closest to them. They could not claim him, these maddened ghosts of Hamur's victims, so they claimed the warm-smelling blood of the beasts—

Fangs tore. Yellow eyes flamed. The leopards became a single mass of awful, heaving flesh. Spotted hides ran pink with blood.

Presently the tangle fell in upon itself, stilled. The last beast twitched and lay unmoving. The black cloud was gone.

Brak wiped sweat out of his eyes. He took a staggering step.

The largest of the leopards rose up, hide running with blood, entrails hanging out—*and looked at him.*

The leopard's maw opened. Brak saw wet red fangs. The leopard gave a cry, but it was not the cry of a wounded beast.

From the leopard's maw came that same lusting shriek of the victims—

Possessed, the leopard leaped.

Brak swung his broadsword as the hot, stinking animal landed on him. *I kill the dead,* Brak's brain howled, not understanding; there was no time to understand. There was time only to fall and avoid the tearing claws. He leaped away as the leopard dropped. He rolled, jumped up. He swung and lopped off the great head with a smashing, pulping sound.

Another was coming now, racing through the litter of treasure, dead and alive at the same time. Brak plunged his sword into its flank, pulled the sword, rammed it in again, fended slashing claws, struck, struck—

The four remaining leopards came on, the voices of the walls howling from their jaws. Brak's broadsword flashed and arced, back and forth, over and down, spraying blood—

When at last he stopped, he was drenched red from head to foot.

He uttered a grunt from deep in his belly. His lips cracked apart in a smile of utter bestiality.

The last of Hamur's leopards lay twitching in its own intestines. Distantly, distantly a thousand damned voices went crying off to the depths of the earth. Vanquished.

A grinding sound reached his ears. Even as he swung to seek the source, he knew what he would see. The stained walls of Hamur's chamber began to show cracks, rifts. Dust showered down. Brak had only an instant in which to seek shelter beneath the overturned throne chair.

The haunted walls, cleansed at last of their possession, crumbled and rocked. They split and sagged in many places, shearing apart, crashing inward, block after block, *crash upon crash upon crash*—

When Brak crawled out from beneath the throne chair much later, he wondered that breath still blew in his lungs at all. Fortunately the great chair's back had shielded him reasonably well. Because of the chair's position at the center of the chamber he had escaped the fall of all but a few of the tumbling blocks. All around the perimeter of the chamber, mounds of rubble were heaped high. Had the chair been near any part of the wall, he would surely have been crushed.

To his left he spied a section of wall that had fallen and noticed with a shudder that it was one of the sec-

tions upon which he had hacked the cross of the Nestorians. The cross-mark was intact.

He turned his eyes away quickly, fearing the power his barbarian's mind did not understand.

Weak, he picked his way through the rubble. About half of the circular wall had crumbled. Many large sections had dropped out of the roof. As he moved through the treasure, he felt the very floor sway. Another huge block came crashing down from overhead, driving up the dust as it crushed ornaments and shattered jewels beneath it.

Cool, misty air was sweeping into the chamber, washing off the rotted stink.

He gathered up as many items of treasure as he could carry—seven pieces. Then he stumbled down the staircase, down the long corridors, and across the drawbridge.

Mirande awaited him. She no longer seemed even remotely beautiful but old and haggard. Her hair tossed in the wind like a nest of white and black snakes.

Behind her, but at some distance, were unwelcome visitors: nearly the entire population of the village, including Yarah the Bull and Friar Benedic.

Mirande threw her arms around Brak's neck. He shook his mighty shoulders, working free. He walked toward the crowd, ignoring their gasps, their signs against the evil eye. He was a hideous figure, his long braid blood matted, his lion hide red smeared, his limbs and chest and face all scarlet. He dumped the seven jeweled pieces at the feet of the astonished Nestorian.

Mirande ran at him and raked her nails down his back. He spun, snarling.

"The spoil is mine!" the woman breathed. "It belonged to my father. Our bargain—"

"The bargain," Brak returned, "was for me to bring forth Hamur's treasure. There was nothing said as to how much. Well, there is Hamur's treasure—" He kicked an emerald-studded cup. "—and the remainder is inside, safe to be taken now." Ignoring her strange, hateful stare, he turned to the Nestorian. "Priest, the sign you bear—" He reached toward the small stone cross in Benedic's hand, but did not touch it. "—has a power I do not understand. But I saw the power work inside the palace. It drove back the demons that would have taken me for their own. So the spoil is yours. I won it and I claim the right to do with it as I will. If times are lean, use it to buy grain for this town. Although these people gawked at me on the block, still I think they're better folk than this woman who would hoard her last dinsha rather than share them to ease the misery of her fellows." He turned and looked hard at Mirande through the mist of pain troubling his eyes. "You're snared in your own bargain, woman. I brought forth Hamur's treasure, and now I'll go free."

With a cry Mirande jumped at him. There was a tiny curved dagger in her fist.

Brak stumbled back, off-balance. Someone barked his name. Mirande's knife hand swept down, straight at his chest—

And then, strangely, she twisted aside. She fell past him, onto the seven pieces of treasure. The blade of her knife struck a sliver casque all crusted with rubies, glanced off, dropped from her hand—

An arrow stood straight up from the center of her back.

Brak shouldered into the crowd. He seized a lance carried by one of the footmen of Yarah the Bull. The man uttered a startled gasp, caught by surprise. Brak turned and hurled the lance high and far.

On a ruined parapet of the palace above the moat the slaver Zaldeb stood up very straight, almost on tiptoes, it seemed. Then he turned slightly. All in the crowd could see the lance that had been driven into him. It had entered his breastbone and pierced out at his back.

Lurching forward, Zaldeb dropped his bow. He pitched over and crashed down into the dry moat. Rats came squealing up over the moat's rim, to run away into the mist.

Brak wiped his forearm down across his eyes. Then he looked at Yarah the Bull.

"I want a place to wash. I want a pony to carry me on my way to Khurdisan." He sucked in a breath. "There is no one who doubts my freedom to go—?"

"No one," said Friar Benedic, a strange expression on his face.

"By the gods, no one!" exclaimed Yarah the Bull, puffing as he dismounted and stumped forward. "My house is open to you, outlander. The humble animal on which I ride is yours for the taking." Then with a covetous glance at the pieces of treasure that could still be seen under Mirande's body, the governor walked toward the drawbridge of the palace of Hamur of a Thousand Claws. By the time he reached it, he was running.

Suddenly the crowd rushed forward too, shouting, laughing, man knocking against man in haste to reach the spoil. Brak watched the mob disappear, howling, into the ruins.

Smiling in an empty way, he reached down and tangled his fingers in Mirande's hair. He pulled her body off the seven pieces, and rolled it aside, saying to Benedic, the one man who had remained behind:

"There is blood enough on it already, I think."

Climbing onto the scrawny gray horse of Yarah the Bull, Brak the barbarian rode down the hillside toward the village. With a last look at the palace of Hamur the priest followed.

GHOUL'S GARDEN

1

The dappled woodlands were a refreshing contrast with the sere, poverty-ridden country which the big barbarian had quitted three moons back, having been enslaved, then freed—by dint of his own strength—after facing the demons in Prince Hamur's enchanted palace.

Here there was no thought of the dead woman, the dead slaver, the leopards, the green-slimed treasure. Here, instead, his pony ambled along in the shifting light of a mild sun falling through crimson-leafed trees.

The breeze washed him with its sweetness. Up in a tree a glittering bird inclined its head and rilled at the riding man, who was huge and strong-looking and wore a lion-hide garment around his middle.

The pony loafed down the barely passable track through the woods. The big man rode with rude grace, his long yellow braid bobbing against his back in hoof-rhythm.

The barbarian had worked hard for the lithe little pony. The pony represented mobility; the big man's chance, again, to ride on. For despite the demons and other terrifying circumstances which he had encountered since his banishment from the high steppes, the wild lands of the north, he was, inevitably, bound to seek his fortune in the warm climes of Khurdisan far southward.

A warm, mellow afternoon. His scars, which sometimes ached in the rain, were healing. His eyes were easy, his mouth relaxed. So when the cry came, round a murky, thicketed bend just ahead, he drew up tight, clutched the rope rein, then let his shoulders slump again.

Some of the quick fire seeped from his eyes. He'd heard a cackle of macabre laughter, no more.

Still—laughter? In the middle of a forest in which he hadn't seen so much as a peasant for several leagues?

The cry came again. Brak the barbarian nudged his pony with his knees. "Wrong," he muttered. "That's a yell of hurt." But uttered, his mind tagged on, by one who squealed easily.

The cry split the wood again.

"Up and look, little one," he said to the pony. It picked up its hoofs, jumping some brambles. The shining bird flew away with a scream. Then Brak heard another sound. A soughing and whipping, as of strong winds through the trees.

The pony trotted around the bend. There the trees thickened over, so that it grew suddenly chilly, and Brak had trouble making out details of the scene revealed to him. When he did, he hauled back on the pony's rope and boomed a laugh.

A short distance ahead along the track a man whose gray habit proclaimed him a priest of the cult of Nestoriamus hung upside down in the air, one ankle wrapped round by the end of a supple branch of a great gnarled tree whose bark had a peculiar purplish shine, as of ichor oozing through from the heartwood.

The priest thus caught, dangling and thrashing like a snared animal, had the hem of his inverted robe hanging around his head like a bell. His face was hidden. His squeal sounded again. Something in Brak's middle turned over.

"A coward's wail," he grumbled, and it distressed

him no little. He had been occasionally perplexed and even awed by the religious pratings of the disciples of the ecstatic goatherd, Nestoriamus. But he had never met a friar yet—and he'd encountered several—who was not stern stuff. This one yelped and kicked. Well, there were always exceptions. Also, Brak noted, Nestorians wore underdrawers.

In the act of urging his pony onward, he noticed two more things.

Another person was present, frantically trying to tug the Nestorian down from the tree. A woman. Possibly young. She wore a coarse, gaudy skirt and blouse. Green necklaces of stone circled her neck. Her hair flashed deep red in a sunbar and looked slatternly.

And the tree—nameless gods!

The tree was *breathing*.

A sticky maw opened and shut, opened and shut at the junction where three main branches formed the trunk. The wind-sigh came from no air currents through the woodland but from that sucking, toothless mouth.

And the creeperlike branch that had wrapped itself around the friar's ankle was bending, writhing, flexing—as if to swing the priest over so that the tree could make a meal.

Suddenly cold, Brak kicked the pony hard. He reached back, unslung the broadsword from where he'd lashed it across his muscled back with a length of gut. His fingers broke the loose knot, and he had the hilt in his huge-fingered hand. He rode down the dim track noisily, as the confusion at the tree continued.

The woman was young. Another bar of light into which she turned revealed it. And she was much painted. As she spun, she saw help. Letting go of the priest's arm, she screamed like a harpy and gestured.

The priest continued to wail. Here and there on the tree Brak saw shining globular fruits hanging, black skins glowing like waxed ebon—

And the maw opened, shut, opened, shut, noisy as a windstorm.

He reined up. In the gloom he perceived a slash of color. Something ran down the priest's leg from the place where the creeper clutched.

Something that shone in the sunshine. Shone red.

"Stand aside, woman," Brak shouted, off the pony and running. "I'll cut him down."

So saying, he leaned in and raised his broadsword high, doublehanding the hilt for a better blow. He felt the impact of the wench's breast, large, soft, as she stumbled out of his way. He smelled her cheap, not unpleasing scent.

The roar of the maw grew louder, it seemed, louder and more angry. From within the bell of the robe hanging down around his head, the priest kept on screaming intermittently. The line of blood reached his knee, trickled on down his thigh toward his drawers.

"Another arm—!" That was the wench shrilling. But Brak didn't realize what she meant till a rough, writhing thing lashed, *smack,* across his chest, then crawled—*crawled*—up to his throat in an eye-blink.

The creeper wrapped round and round, constricted.

Brak's rage came out a growl. He planted his great legs, the yellow braid and the lion tail whipsawing as he tried to wrench free of the tightening creeper. The creeper clutched his neck all the tighter. Fireballs with pointed arms burst inside his head, and there was intense pain.

Unseeing, he hacked down. He felt the broadsword skate off the creeper's rough bark. His eye sockets were afire. Darkness pressed in from the corners of his mind.

Raging, full of red hate, he swung maniacally, chopping the broadsword from the right, from the left, the right—

Abruptly the creeper cracked.

The maw keened in unholy rage, the wind sound sharpening to a shriek. Brak leaped back as two more creepers dropped twitching toward his face. One rasped his cheek, but he eluded it. The severed creeper round his throat poured foul pasty brown stuff from its cut end. But it did not release.

The brown odor rose sickeningly. The big barbarian dropped the broadsword and tore at the creeper with both hands, tore and tore, wounding his own flesh with his yellow-thick nails. He couldn't stop. The compulsion to get the awful thing away from him was like a bewitchment.

At last he broke the hold. Beneath its bark the creeper felt alive, muscled. He stamped on it when it fell, then picked it up and threw it away like a still-writhing serpent. Panting, he dove for his broadsword as another creeper, then two, lashed at his shoulder. He dodged away.

"What kind of a hell's tree—?" he half screamed to the girl.

"Witch-apple," she cried back. "The friar and I were traveling together—we walked too close—"

The friar was still howling like one peering into the infernal regions a last time. Strange, unmanly behavior for one of the order, Brak thought again. He wiped his mouth, lowered his head, stared balefully at the dangling priest.

A second creeper had fixed itself round the man's scrawny middle, and slowly, slowly, while the tree-

maw roared like the wind, the Nestorian was being drawn up and over to the place where the three mighty branches joined.

Still hurting from the clutch of the creeper on his neck, Brak let the red wrath of the berserker claim him completely. He charged in, hacking and mauling with the sword until he smelled the putrid brown paste dripping from hacked branches.

He severed the creeper round the priest's waist, then the one round his ankle. The man dropped, nearly smashing his brains out on a large stone.

The priest flopped over, his head, balding and horse-jawed, popping out of his tangled robes. Then, on hands and knees, he scuttled away from the demon tree. Brak had a glimpse of moistened eyes turned in fury at the slatternly girl.

"You—slut," the priest panted. "You didn't—" Gulping air. "—act swiftly enough. I—" Gulping, gulping. "—might have died!"

Then he was up, twisting the girl's arm. Over his shoulder he saw Brak glaring. He let go, pale and sullen-faced. The girl cried out.

Maddened by its loss, the witch-apple thrashed its creepers and flailed two, four, six at the big barbarian to seize him from all sides.

Brak jumped high, cut through the nearest one, dodged beneath another—and knew he'd never escape the evil growth using only the iron of his sword. He flung the blade away. It clanged on a rock, making the pony start.

Brak bent, grunted in pain and effort as he locked hands on the stone on which the priest had almost dashed his head open. A creeper slid toward his right foot. He stamped on it. Another reached to twine round his yellow braid. The big barbarian jerked his head aside. Tearing some hair, he got free.

Then he shoved the immensely heavy rock up high over his head and ran two, three, four stumbling steps. His arm muscles hurt from the weight. But he kept going until he could drop the rock down into the tree's maw.

The rock fell out of sight. For a moment all the creepers relaxed, trailed to the ground. Then, abruptly, came the most hideous sound the big barbarian had ever heard.

Deep within itself the tree was roaring and grinding, making a noise of choking, of anguish—

The maw opened out to full width and the witch-apple began to vomit up a geyser of the brown paste streaked with yellow.

Exhausted, Brak hid his eyes behind his forearm and whirled and smashed into the priest and the wench.

"Run! Run fast!"

Somehow he recovered his broadsword. Swinging wide of the track through brambles that raked his legs, he dragged the pony by its rope until he was past the witch-apple. Great slabs of slimy bark were falling from the tree as it shook itself and made that awful sound within its guts. The creepers lashed the ground like whips, hitting so furiously that they broke, oozing brown pasty stuff. The maw was vomiting up brilliant yellow fluid now, thick as molten gold.

Blundering ahead, pushing priest and wench down the track while he pulled his pony, the big barbarian didn't look back more than once.

2

They camped together at sunfall. Not exactly willingly; simply because they had been thrown into each other's company. The wood grew quickly dark.

They were in a glade. Brak took eager comfort from the fire he struck with flints and metal which the girl produced from a large, much-patched carry bag. The barbarian couldn't recall her picking up the bag when they fled the witch-apple, but obviously she had. And she placed great importance on it, too.

His eyes grew amused as the girl replaced the iron and flints, then rummaged among the other items she'd spread out: a little skin wine flacon; a cloth bundle which proved to contain a somewhat moldy loaf of unleavened bread; various items of clothing and cheap jewelry; and several small stone pots with skin covers. There were pink and scarlet smears all over the pots. The colors matched those of the girl's smeared mouth and cheeks.

A much-painted woman, he mused as the fire warmed his outstretched hands. Not old, but hard-used by the world. She was handsome. Had a fine figure. And he rather liked her quick, capable way of moving. As she bent, her blouse fell away from her breasts.

Brak grunted to himself. He had traveled alone a long while. An image of Rhea, the queen he loved, gentled through his mind then. But it did not stay overlong.

"—in here somewhere," she was saying. "This is all

in the world I have for belongings." Out came more articles of clothing. Something fell from them, glaring by firelight.

A dagger.

Off in the distance a loonlike cry rang through the woods. She kept talking:

"I carry a pot of the soothing paste because we often played small towns where there was no leech or cutter. Whenever one of our company was hurt in a play-fight on stage, I became the leech, required to tend and dress—"

"Can't you stop that yammer, woman?"

The unpleasant voice grated across the flames. It stirred a wrath in Brak that he could not explain. The Nestorian sat yonder, his spindly leg thrust out. His wound had clotted. The dried blood looked ugly.

"The girl's trying to find something to tend your hurt, priest," Brak said. "Show a little gratitude. You've done nothing but complain since we left that accursed tree."

The priest's perpetually moist eyes threw back points of firelight. "I need no lessons in deportment from an unlettered—"

"By the gods," said the girl with a sigh. "He *saved* you, Friar Hektor. I couldn't have done it."

Friar Hektor glanced away. "I believe I thanked the outlander back on the road."

Brak grunted. The Nestorian had not, but he said nothing.

"Well, patience," the girl said, hauling out more apparel from the bag. Brak laughed out loud.

She raised her head, the green stones of her necklaces shining against her cleavage. She smiled. It softened the hardness of her and stirred Brak deep down. Friar Hektor made another querulous sound.

"Here, holy man." Brak tore off a chunk of the moldy bread, tossed it across the fire. "Nourish yourself." A gesture to the cross hanging from a cord at the priest's waist. The cross was gray stone, with arms of equal length. "Or keep busy speaking with that nameless one all you gray-robes worship."

Friar Hektor couldn't help catching the dislike in Brak's voice. And, in truth, the big barbarian couldn't help himself either. The Nestorian seemed a mean man, soured by the world.

Hektor retorted, "Have a care in what you say about the gods. Blasphemy is—"

"I don't fear reprisal from your god," Brak said, shrugging.

"Nor from any, I suspect," said the priest with contempt. "It's obvious you worship your own thick arms and that filthy instrument of murder you carry."

Useless to carp back and forth with such a spoiled, twisted specimen, Brak thought. Yet the man's meanness so provoked him that he reached out and stroked the broadsword and said:

" 'Tis something indisputably real—which can't always be said for the power of this god of yours. Back there, his power seemed of little use in saving your life. I know your god exists—but is he always present when he's needed? I know my sword is. I see to it. And when I ram it down the mouth of some troublemaking fool, I have no doubt of the outcome of the deed. I wonder if that can be said of a god who may or may not be at your service when called—"

Friar Hektor was visibly shaken by Brak's cruel, joking tone. The last words flushed him with anger. "I have thanked you once, and once is enough for—"

"Oh, bother!"

The friar turned toward the girl. "What's that you say?"

The girl jumped up, a stone pot in her hand. "Surely he has a name. Be gracious enough to use it."

Then she tossed her deep red hair. Rounding the fire, she glanced obliquely at Brak.

"What is your name, anyway?"

He told them and explained that he was a wanderer, traveling by the most convenient roadways south, toward Khurdisan.

"My name's Shana." Kneeling, she began to apply a pale blue paste to the priest's wound. He winced and complained, but she paid no attention, continuing to Brak: "This is hardly a convenient road, is it? This country is so desolate. I hate it. Besides the witch-apples that grow all through here, tales say there are many thieves and brigands who roam these parts. Oh, be still, priest!" she finished.

Friar Hektor ceased his clack, ugly eyed.

"I've seen no one rich enough to rob," Brak grinned. "Certainly I am not."

Shana smiled back, a warm, softening smile. "Nor I. In truth I only took this route because it's the most direct to Thenngil."

He repeated the name, as a question.

"A province some leagues south," she said. "I have a cousin there. A farmer with a good wife and a brood of young. I—" Her voice broke a moment. "I hope to live with them till I decide what's next for me. I'll work to earn my keep, of course," she added firmly.

"What's next, you say? Something important is recently over?"

"Our troupe is no more."

"Troupe?"

Hektor said, "She means she was one of a company

of traveling players. As I told you before, girl, you're better off out of that business. 'Tis fit only for whores."

"Thank you very much," she replied, "but I've worked the roads ten years now, ever since my breasts grew, and I've never offered myself casually, nor sold myself to any man. Those men that I have—well, that is—there must be—"

After a hesitation she bent to tying off the strip of rag which she was using to bandage the priest's leg. She finished softly:

"There must be a liking."

"What happened to your troupe?" Brak wanted to know. "I have never seen a play-show, if that's what you call them. But I've heard of them."

Shana explained that several towns back the troupe master, one Onselm, had become involved with a woman whose husband returned unexpectedly and, in a duel, slew the actor. "He was our genius. Our teacher, our keeper of the purse. It was he who argued with the locals over the price of our engagements. Without him the troupe lost heart. At the last village, Megaro—" Something sick lay in her eyes then. Some tainted memory that made her shudder. "—we decided to disband, for we all realized we were little good without Onselm. He'd worked the roads forty years and more."

Brak waved a chunk of bread. "How did you two come together, then?"

"We met on the road back there, before the wood," Hektor answered, pushing the girl's hand away as she tried to adjust his bandage. He stood, groaning. He was, Brak saw, a small man. "Since we were going the same way, south, we decided we would be safer together."

Brak tried to hide his continued nasty amusement.

Hektor obviously doubted the wisdom of his own decision.

"Your purpose," asked Brak, "being to avoid those thieves and brigands she mentioned?"

"Really, it's true—we have nothing worth stealing," Shana said, opening the flacon. She drank like a man, over her arm.

She wiped the flacon on her skirt and passed it to Brak. He put his lips to it and tasted the pleasing afterscent of hers.

Shana crouched down beside the fire, continuing, "But even though we're penniless, it's wise to be careful. The woods people have lived so long with plundering and hurting, so the tales say, they do it for the pleasure now, whether there's booty or not. In numbers—"

"Safety," Brak nodded. But he wondered again at the awful, frightened way she eyed the dark trees beyond the ring of light.

The trees whispered in the wind. The night was growing bone-cold. "Where are you bound, friar, besides south?" he asked.

"On a missionary journey." That was that.

Shana helped herself to more wine after Brak passed it back. She offered the flacon to the priest. He raised his hand, as though the offer, like the flacon, was unclean. The girl shrugged, drank a third time, shivered. Brak wondered at that too, until she said:

"Now that we've a little quiet, there is something I must say to you both, in case you want to go on separately."

Hektor scowled. "Something you haven't told me?"

"Y—yes." The wind had flushed her cheeks. "I wanted to but—somehow, I couldn't bring myself—"

"Weakness," muttered the priest. His gaze accused

her of causing him more unpleasantness. She pressed her palms against her thighs and kept her head bent as if she were afraid of their faces:

"One of the chief reasons I fled alone, by night, from Megaro town, was that a—a certain man watched us play our last performance there. When it was done, he came to find me. He said—" Again she trembled. "—he said he wanted me."

Picking at his teeth, Brak remarked, "Doesn't a woman find it pleasant to be told she's attractive?"

Up came her head, the dark red hair aglitter. There was a hellish fear in her eyes.

"You haven't seen this man."

"Some glutted old satyr, no doubt," Hektor sniffed. "Offering you a few dinshas for—"

"No. He told me—" Her hands pressed white on her legs. "—he told me he would offer me nothing. That he need offer me nothing because he was a wizard."

In the cooling night the lonely bird sounded again. Brak's spine crawled without him willing it. He said nothing. Shana went on:

"He called himself Pom."

Hektor snorted. "No fancy thaumaturgical titles?"

Shana stared into the fire as if staring at the unspeakable. Her voice was barely audible:

"Just Pom. A man no taller than—" She indicated her breasts. "—here. With a curious child's body, thin and odd, as though it had all been broken in the past and mended together wrong. Or never put together right in the first place. But his head was this large." Her hands spread apart. "With not a hair on it, giving him the look of some ghastly little boy. His eyes—you have never seen such eyes—round and milky-gray. Huge." Suddenly, watching the fire, she bowed her head and bit the back of her hand.

Even Hektor found nothing to say, for the fear in the glade was like a poison. Presently Shana glanced up again. She said:

"There's little more to tell, except that I slipped away from him. He seemed a poor man, with a threadbare robe. But he said wizards did not need fine apparel, for they controlled a secret, more beautiful world. He had a black pony, I remember. Lashed to its back was an old leathern trunk. Not large, just very old. He said that if I would lay with him, he'd open the trunk and show me mystical things. A garden where the air smelled of balm, and it was ever twilight, and golden metal birds sang in trees beside a pool full of diamonds—"

She stared at Brak, as if seeking protection. "He described it as beautiful and yet, somehow, I knew it was—an evil place."

Quickly she drank again.

Friar Hektor began to finger his stone cross and eye the surrounding dark. Brak knew that without a doubt they were in the company of a coward.

"Well," he said as lightly as he could, "I'm bound south too. We'll all go together for a ways, and damn the wizard." A moment later, "You don't think he followed you, do you?"

Shana's eyes were empty. "I have no reason to think he did. Except—the lust in him—so crippled, wanting a whole woman so badly—I suppose it's possible that he might—"

"Well," Brak said again, shrugging, "I've this to protect us." He crouched down near the slowly dying fire and slapped his broadsword. Then he pointed to Hektor. "And our holy man has his little cross, and that should pull us through. Anyway, your wizard was probably just some sickly beggar ragging you with scare tales of an empty trunk."

Shana looked at Brak the barbarian once more and tried to believe.

"Yes, you could be right. Yes, I'm glad you said that. Now I can sleep. We'll travel on together."

Somehow she found yet another item—a frowzy sleeping rug—inside the bag. She rolled up in it, giving Brak one final, thankful glance. He thought briefly of her body beneath her cheap, bright clothes, then decided this was the wrong time. With the sword iron against his belly he settled down.

Friar Hektor was mumbling some incantation or other to his Nameless God. That kept Brak awake awhile, annoyed. Finally the priest quieted, as did the flames. Silence deepened in the glade.

Brak turned this way, that, left side, right side, left again. He heard similar restless noises from Shana. But at last these, too, ceased. He fell into a thin, uneasy slumber.

He had a dream.

He was lying rigid, on his back, unmoving and unable to move, staring up through moon-fired treetops at a great beast, a black horse, thundering down the sky in silence with a stunted rider on its back.

The hoofs of the beast slashed the air, but it made no sound in its passing, only trailed thin streams of fire from its nostrils. It loomed larger than the moon a moment, then passed on into the silvered clouds, southward.

Dazed, Brak sat up. He clutched his sword and nicked himself on the cutting edge. He said an oath and sucked his finger. Then, almost afraid of what he would see, he raised his eyes—

And saw the same moon-drenched treetops.

Had he dreamed? *Had* he?

In the silvered sky two faint parallel trails, like pink vapor, seemed to be vanishing. The cold night air had a sulphurous stench, as though the world had opened and belched forth some of its evil; evil that now lingered to taint, to promise—unspeakable things.

He slept badly the rest of the night.

3

Morning brought gloom, and rain.

Thunder smote the forest. Long blue streaks of lightning crisscrossed the sky. The downpour continued an inordinately long time, during which Brak was forced to squat scowling in the cover of the trees, rain dripping off his matted yellow brows. His eyes strayed now and then to Shana. She was as disgusted as he by Friar Hektor's constant complainings.

Eventually the rain let off to a drizzle. They agreed to resume their journey.

Friar Hektor demanded that he be allowed to ride Brak's pony. The barbarian gave him a hand up, rougher than necessary, and took pleasure when the priest winced.

"I meant to offer you the animal," Brak said. He turned his back and set off down the track, yellow braid swinging.

The rain continued intermittently, and the forest gradually thinned. The sky grew dark again, an early nightfall because of the fast-flying clouds that only occasionally split to shine silver from the hidden sun. Brak stopped slogging along the muddy track and held up a hand, ears all sharp.

"A strange sound—" he began.

Shana came up beside him, lugging her carry bag over her shoulder. Her old, worn slipper skidded on a mud-slimed, half-buried rock. She crashed against Brak, exclaiming in embarrassment.

With her free hand she pushed back her limp, wet

hair. For a moment their eyes held. Then the big barbarian turned away again. He wasn't easy in such situations, and he felt unmanned by what he was sure the girl saw in his eyes: naked admission of his feelings.

"We're coming to a river," Friar Hektor said as Brak's pony plopped up behind them. "Anyone can hear that."

The barbarian stifled a retort and, as he did, Shana put in, "From the noise it's running fast. Probably because of the rain. We won't cross tonight, I'll wager."

Somehow Brak felt uneasy about that. He signed them forward, and in a short time they emerged in lowering night on a weedy bank.

The river was not wide. But it ran at furious speed over treacherous-looking rocks directly in front of them. Dark had all but fallen. Brak perceived details but dimly.

Foams and whorls of swift white water barred their path. On the far side he glimpsed the barest suggestion of the track continuing up among the boulders into more rugged terrain.

Brak crouched, tracing a forefinger in the mud. He dipped the finger down into an indentation.

"There's the track of a hoof here. More than one. But how many passed here earlier, and whether they went across or turned back, I can't tell. It could be one rider, it could be several."

He slashed the drizzle off his forehead. "If it weren't so cursed dark—"

But cursing was no use. The hoofprints were lost. It grew blacker moment by moment. The wind was picking up, chilling him deep.

He raised his head, stared out across the water that boiled with faint luminescence. "Obviously, since the track comes down to here, there's a ford somewhere about. But at night—"

"If you think I intend to risk myself on such a chancy crossing when we've no light, you're mistaken," Friar Hektor exclaimed.

Brak stood up, wiped his free hand on the lion skin at his waist. He took a harder grip on the hilt of his broadsword. The iron blade was resting across one brawny shoulder, point aimed behind him.

"We won't subject your noble person to such hazards, priest. We'll make camp on this side and cross with the light."

"We'll camp if we can find a dry place," Shana said wearily.

"Up the bank—" Brak began, swinging that way.

And saw, for the first time, a human figure silhouetted against a rectangle of deep, smudgy orange, not far to his left down the riverside.

With a start he realized it was a man. The man was standing in a cottage doorway with firelight behind him. A man of good physical size, too. Well set up, with a large head topped by curly hair. The man raised his hand and hallooed:

"Travelers?"

"Aye," Brak shouted back. "Travelers seeking shelter from the rain."

"Come this way; my house is yours."

Friar Hektor hissed through his teeth. "The girl spoke of cruel men in these wild parts. Foresters who prey upon—"

Brak's vile oath shut the priest up. "I'm sick of your carping and your damn dissatisfaction, priest. That's a big man yonder, but I see no more than one of him, and I'm tired and hungry, and I'll trade the risks for a chance at his fire. You may be terrified of him but I'm not. Sit out here in safety and misery all night if it pleases you, but in case it does, haul your shanks off my pony. He deserves shelter in the lee of the house."

With that, Brak grabbed the pony's rein and jerked.

Friar Hektor was forced to slide quickly to the ground before being dumped off by the pony's sudden forward motion. For a moment Hektor's face was lit by the dim glare from the cottage.

The Nestorian barely stood to Brak's neck. In the small man's upturned eyes the barbarian saw the sad, foolish loathing of the small for the larger. With his broadsword over his shoulder and his pony rope in the other hand, he plodded toward the cottage.

He was wary; wary but not alarmed. Yet there was something, *something*, prickling uneasily at the back of his mind–

"That's sensible talk at last," Shana said as she fell in step beside him. Friar Hektor resumed his grumbling. But he followed.

"Welcome, welcome," the tall man said as they approached. He stepped back into the small, rude house, which had a reed roof. Up there smoke crawled from a pot set among the reeds.

The man turned sidewise. Firelight fell athwart his face. Something about that face made Brak's mind prickle even more.

The man was young, with broad shoulders, a small waist, and a handsome, tanned face. A man of strength, vigor; a man open to the weather. Nothing there of which to be suspicious. Yet Brak didn't like him.

He felt the dislike even more strongly when the man smiled at Shana with unhidden interest. The man did pause long enough to point around the cottage corner and say to the barbarian, "There's a bale of woods grass somewhere back there. The pony can feed."

Then he stepped even farther back inside, executing a half bow. Decidedly odd behavior for one living so far apart from others, Brak thought. Even he, an unlettered offspring of the wild northern lands, had been among civilized peoples long enough to know that.

The man touched Shana's arm as she passed inside. He smiled, a wide, white, perfect smile of charm and ease.

"Come in, please, and get yourselves warm and dry. My name's Yan. I'm a woodcutter. I see few strangers. I'm glad of the company."

Brak located the woods grass bale and left the pony tied and chomping. He thought he heard another animal stirring out in the weeds where the rain pattered but saw nothing, so he headed back inside. His teeth were chattering from the cold. He was more tired than he had imagined. Something ran around in his head, a peculiar thought—

A woodcutter, a woodcutter.

And to whom does he sell his wood, leagues from anyone or anything?

The absence of rain and the sudden curl of firewarmth against his skin made him abandon the bothersome thought. He slung down his broadsword as Friar Hektor made for the only stool in the one-room house. There were few other furnishings: a rude table, a pallet of blankets laid upon straw; an empty blackened kettle hanging from an iron prong beside the fireplace. Yan the woodcutter seemed to have no store of clothing, not even any personal belongings. There were cobwebbings up in the ceiling corners. Brak watched a fat yellow-black spider crawling in its web, then glanced back as Yan spoke to the priest in a courteous tone:

"I believe the lady has first right to sit, father. Would you be so good—?"

Grumbling, Hektor got up. With a little smile that hid her weariness, Shana thanked Yan and sat down. She kicked off her slippers and toasted the bottoms of her dirty feet.

Yan bustled around, drawing the table near her while Brak stood like a rock, watching Shana's grateful expression and the way the woodcutter's dark eyes kept returning to her face.

"Here—wine—cheese—I eat a simple meal at night, but you're all welcome to finish it. There is still plenty, I think."

Friar Hektor extended his hand. "Pass the wine."

Yan did, without so much as a murmur. Something smelled all wrong to Brak.

Perhaps it was only his simple mind. Or perhaps it was another feeling he hated to admit—

Shana was hugging her knees now, feet drawn up on the stool's rung. Yan held out a slab of cheese. She accepted with perfect pleasure.

Brak had seldom seen such a handsome fellow as the woodcutter. He couldn't help disliking the way Shana seemed taken with him.

"Tell me who you are and where you're bound," Yan said as he seated himself on the hearthstone. He wore tight trousers, woodsman's boots, a tunic over a coarse shirt. He seemed elegant of speech for a man who lived far apart from cities.

"My name's Shana. I was part of a traveling troupe—" And she was launched into an explanation of her decision to journey to the farm of her cousin. She mentioned the unwelcome attentions of a man as having contributed to her plan, but she said nothing about a wizard, nor named him. Brak thought he recognized the fear in her eyes again, but just a flicker. She was fighting to conceal it.

Then, a moment later:

She's trying to conceal it so he'll not think her simple and foolish.

Brak felt hot, wrathful. This tough, capable young woman had attracted him more than he cared to admit. He disliked Yan's attentive stare more and more each moment. He felt cloddish in the man's presence.

Suddenly Yan glanced up, his eyes keen as he looked at the big barbarian.

"And you? The lion skin marks you some kind of outlander."

"Called Brak, and bound south." He reached for cheese, unwilling and unable to say more.

"Are you quite warm enough?" Yan inquired of Shana.

"Yes, thank you. The fire's very pleasant."

"If there's anything here to make you more comfortable—"

Yan gestured to take in the room. Why did it look so unused? So dusty in the corners? The rain pattered softly, steadily, on the reed roof.

"No, you're most kind," Shana smiled. Gods, how Brak hated this handsome young buck of a sudden.

He was struggling for something to say when he heard a noise outside. The quick, fearful whinny of his pony.

Yan looked around, sharply. Brak's belly went tight as the pony started stamping. He left his broadsword leaning against the wall and went outside, catching the pony's head rope just as the animal trotted past the front of the cottage, running away.

Brak tugged. The pony quieted a little. The barbarian rubbed his hand up and down the warm muzzle, talking soothing nonsense.

The pony let its head down and stood still. Brak blinked in the rain. He heard another noise from the rear of the little house.

Something compelled him to quiet. He edged round the cottage corner and slid along the wall until he could make out a shape looming in the weeds—

Brak crouched. A moment later he let out his breath. His reaction had been unwarranted. What stood there was nothing more than a horse. A horse of good size, true, and powerful looking. But nothing uncommon. He took another step forward, his hardened soles sliding in mud.

The horse tossed its head back and snapped at him.

Brak stopped. He stared at the beast a long moment. Black, it was. Black as the raining night.

Then, as the barbarian's eyes grew more accustomed to the dark, he noted something bulking from the horse's back. He edged a step closer.

The horse tossed its long, tangled mane. A vicious animal. Brak made a sound in his throat, a primitive sound, a sound of threat. Somehow the beast understood and remained still. Brak recognized the shape jutting up from the horse's back. It was a trunk, strapped in place as if the horse's owner were ready for a swift departure. Not a large trunk, but very old, battered at the corners. A leathern trunk—

"He said if I would lay with him, he'd open the trunk and show me mystical things. A garden where the air smelled of balm, and it was ever twilight—"

Now there was a horror on Brak, the horror of the unknown half glimpsed, and he turned and bolted back to the door of the cottage.

The door was still open. He checked in the dark as the bile of fear rose up in his throat.

Seated against the wall, Friar Hektor had fallen into a doze. Shana perched on her stool by the fire. Between the girl and the doorway Yan the woodsman was reaching for another slab of cheese, his teeth white in a smile, his curly black hair shining. Brak saw Shana's strong, pretty face as through a gauzy curtain—

He saw it through the flesh of Yan's outreaching hand.

The woodsman's hand drew back, carrying a piece of cheese. The barbarian cursed himself for leaving his broadsword inside. So he chose surprise, moving fast, leaping inside the door and to one side, reaching downward.

Yan didn't miss the significance of Brak's outstretched hand. Some of the handsomeness left his face.

"Is there something amiss?"

"Much," Brak growled, broadsword hilt in his grasp. "I don't yet know what, but it's something foul as—"

Crystal-white fire leaped from Yan's hand to the sword. The cottage rang with a sound like a great bell. Brak's head vibrated with pain.

Touched by the fire, the broadsword flew across the room and fell, clattering.

4

Brak seized the rude table, hurled it aside so he could get to Yan. The woodsman's handsome face became strangely distorted. His dark eyes glared. Through Yan's tunic the big barbarian saw the cottage wall in clear detail.

"Shana! Out the door!" Brak yelled as he lunged, hands open, fingers ready for Yan's throat.

The woodsman backed off a step, made another mesmeric pass in the air. A sheet of crystal-white fire blazed up in front of Brak's eyes, hiding everything, and the thunderous bell-like sound pealed inside his head.

The fire seemed to reach inside Brak's brains and broil them. His huge legs turned weak. He collapsed, twitching, on the floor, drool running out of his mouth. Pain was singing in every fiber of him.

When he jammed his palms on the rude plank floor and tried to push up, he was swept with overwhelming nausea and more pain. He could barely keep his eyes open. He had a bleary, sideways view of the room. Through Yan's boots he saw hearth-flames.

The flash of enchanted fire had roused the Nestorian. Mumbling and quavering, Hektor tottered to his feet.

"I smell devils here—the influence of Yob-Haggoth—" His fingers struggled for a grip on the stone cross hanging at his waist.

Yan made a sound of utter hate, leaped and tore at the cross. The cord hanging from Hektor's waist snapped. Shana shrieked as Yan spun and flung the cross into the fire.

A thunderclap, a boil of intense light—the sound and glare smote Brak like a blow. He flopped over on his back, wondering whether he was dying. Somewhere, distantly, he heard a voice—Shana's—now edged with terror and knowing:

"You—you aren't as you seem. You are someone—"

Her words choked off. Brak rolled over on his belly in time to see the woodsman seize the girl by both shoulders.

"Aye," Yan whispered, staring at her with inhumanly bright eyes. "Aye, it's all illusion here. But now I'll show you what I wanted you to see, from that moment I caught sight of you behind the rushlights on the stage in the square."

As Yan spoke, his voice changed, rose up a scale to a ghoulish, scraping squeal, almost childlike, yet with an ugly undertone. Yan's body began to waver, as though glimpsed through a fall of water. Some smoky shape was forming behind it. *Within* it.

In his weakened, pain-wracked state Brak knew the reality of his suspicions then. Knew the truth as Yan flung Shana down so hard that she struck her head on the corner of the overturned table.

Yan dashed to the door. He grew dimmer, more insubstantial with each step. Rain slashed his face as he turned his head, looked back into the cottage. Trying to rise, unable, Brak saw a second head, a second face materialize—

Brak blinked against the pain pulsing through him. When his eyes came open, he glimpsed a small, shriveled body crouched in the door in a curiously broken posture. The apparition wore a plain, threadbare robe. Brak saw a huge hairless head, a delicate nose, a tiny mouth. And immense protruding milky-gray eyes staring and staring at Shana, as though she were naked.

Then Pom the wizard vanished in the rain.

5

"Up," Brak mouthed between his teeth.

He heard Friar Hektor whimpering. He managed to push to all fours, started crawling to his fallen broadsword. He knew, in full horror, the depth of Pom's lust; lust that had driven the wizard to speed ahead of them—that steed in the sky, it had been no dream—and set his snare of illusion.

Brak seemed to be crawling up a great plain at a steep angle. Each movement required immense effort. He stretched out his right hand. The fingers trembled. He closed the fingers around the hilt of his fallen blade—

A yell of pure bestial agony tore out of his mouth.

The broadsword blazed with heat. He tore his hand away, half growling, half whimpering. Pom had enchanted the iron with his crystal fire. Pom had made the blade impossible to wield. Brak lay dazed, helpless a moment—

Footfalls.

The hem of a robe swished past Brak's line of vision. The wizard reappeared before the hearth.

Shana was just beginning to rouse. Tears of terror streaked her cheeks. She recognized her surroundings, tried to struggle up. Pom laid a slippered foot on her neck and held her down while he wrestled his old leathern trunk to the ground.

He was speaking as he tore at the rope ties that held the lid in place, speaking in a childish, demented squeak:

"—told you little of myself, I think. Well, I was born in a dark, wet place under the earth. My mother was a tavern whore. My father was a wizard of some skill, but one—" *Crash,* the trunk lid went back. Those immense milky-gray eyes stood forth from his head, sick with desire. "—one who offended many a fearsome god. For that reason I was born as you see me. Crippled. Cursed. No woman will touch me unless I make her touch me, by surrounding her with the one great magic my father had among his effects at the time of his death."

Out of Brak's vision, Friar Hektor cried, "What kind of debased creature are you? If you've the powers of a thaumaturge as you say, why must you behave like a common clod bent on—on rape?"

"Ah, there's the catch, priest." Pom's tiny blue-veined hands dipped out of sight in the open trunk. For a moment his moist eyes reflected a curious agony. "I am but half a wizard. Even my spell-making powers are cursed and bent crooked like my body. When I tricked you, made you see the woodsman—that was a spell, yes." Pom licked his lips, turned to stare at Shana again. "But I cannot hold the spell when I love a woman." His mouth wrenched. "So I must have a proper setting, you see. A proper enchantment. I've wandered the world a hundred years and more—" Hektor gasped. "—chained in this broken flesh, the mark of the curses laid on my father, and the liquorish heat of my mother's lusts driving me on."

The wizard's eyes glared with hate. "She loved her work, she did. A whore of uncontrollable passions." And then his voice became softer, with an evil sibilance, as he looked yet another time at Shana's body. "We are none of us without flaws, y'see. Not even magicians."

And he whirled his fists up from the trunk, his fingers full of a big, dark silk that seemed to blow and billow out in all directions.

With a snap Pom spread the silk, let it settle to the floor beside the trunk. Brak tried to rise again. He was getting a little of his strength back. Pom cast him a wary glance but didn't seem overly alarmed.

Pom crouched down. He knotted one tiny hand in Shana's deep red hair and pulled her head back.

"No woman I've seen in a year has fired me as you have, my girl. You've the smell of the slut on you. Perhaps that's what excites me." Then, like a carrion-creature, he swooped his mouth on hers.

Shana shrieked. The cry was muffled behind the kiss. Pom broke away. Struggling, he pushed his forearms beneath her, lifted her.

Sweat popped out on his smooth, bulging forehead. His breath came hard as he took a labored step toward the silk lying on the floor. "In my father's garden perhaps you'll find yourself bemused enough to submit. Yes, I rather think you will." With a step he was standing on the edge of the silk.

Instantly he, and Shana in his arms, were gone.

Friar Hektor crab-stepped toward the curiously patterned piece of cloth. His horse-jaw hanging down in horror-struck amazement, the Nestorian put one sandal on the silk.

"Don't touch it!" Brak shouted. "There's some power in it that transports—"

Too late. The priest had both feet on the silk square. He vanished.

6

A dreadful stillness enveloped the cottage. It was broken only by tiny sounds: the fragrant fireplace popping, rain blowing in the open doorway and pattering on the floor, the wind of night snapping the silk where it lay, horror creaking inside Brak's head.

After a long moment he was able to stand. He tottered toward the silk, almost fell upon it, righted himself with a yelp of alarm. Then, carefully, he hunkered and studied the intricate patterning of the material.

It had an order, a design, after all. The basic ground color was a blackish-green. Into this were worked shapes both regular and otherwise, the former being created by lines that ran in from the edges of the silk and intersected one another. The irregular shapes had no clear pattern, were merely positioned here and there.

Of a sudden the barbarian understood. He was staring down at the plan of some sort of garden. The dividing lines were hedges, the irregular shapes pools and grottos.

As he stared at the silk, it seemed that he heard a faint, faraway singing, as of a woman's voice, very sweet, very beguiling. His backbone crawled.

A garden. A flat garden spread before him as if he were a god. As he stared, he thought he saw tiny motes within the strands of silk, two motes in one place, a single mote in another—

Pom and Shana. Hektor.

Alive in a garden of silk.

Despite his terror he knew what must be done. He started for the broadsword again, found it still searing to the touch. A weapon. A weapon! He could not essay it without one—

His eyes fell on Shana's carry bag lumped in a corner.

He pawed through it like a madman until he found the dagger he'd seen in the wood. He thrust the blade into the lion hide at his waist. Then, wobbling but erect, he stumbled to the edge of the silk.

He swallowed, his palms cold-slick with fear. He took a final look at the dying fire and stepped on the cloth.

Singing and dark engulfed him.

7

Overhead stretched a sky of pink and amber broken by long, sculptured clouds of pearl gray. Brak saw the twilight sky above the trimmed top of a hedge that was half a head taller than he. In the distance someone was singing—that seductive, unearthly voice.

Like the hedges that boxed him round, the grass beneath his feet had a glossy blackness in the subtly poisonous light. The garden was a somber, beautiful place. Yet it sickened him in a way he could not explain.

His head filled with a delicious scent that had a subtle, sensuous tinge. Behind him he heard a metallic plashing.

He turned, muscles loosening a little, and without even thinking, he went into the old, wary half crouch of the steppe stalker. There was something animal about the baleful eyes, the ready hands finally draining of their pain, the barbaric lion tail and yellow braid hanging down.

The plashing came from a fountain beside a tile-edged pool. The water pouring from the fountain fell in silver droplets. Shana's words came echoing:

"—and it was ever twilight, and golden metal birds sang beside a pool full of diamonds."

The silvery water did indeed resemble diamonds falling and drifting. A fish swam into view close to the surface, slithery and graceful. The fish regarded Brak with a multicolored faceted eye, then dove away.

Brak began to grunt under his breath, the hate-chant of the hunter. He seemed boxed round by the hedge. But a circuit of the pool showed him a narrow opening.

He eased the dagger into his right hand and slid through sideways. He found himself in another, almost identical area, bordered by hedges. Here, though, a number of trees grew. On a low branch sat one of the golden metal birds, a thing of loveliness that cooed and cooed.

The bird's folded wings reflected the pink and amber of the sky. Listening to the faraway singing, Brak grew drowsy. The woman's voice teased, beckoned, seduced, so that, for a warm, languorous moment, he could only think of one thing—holding a woman in his arms.

Then he remembered Shana's plight. His lips skinned back, ugly again, and he edged past the first of the trees.

Large, opalescent fruits hung from the branches. Brak's belly growled. He plucked down one of the fruits.

It had a soft, yielding skin, and nearly filled his fist. He had the fruit halfway to his mouth when caution checked him.

Instead of eating, he closed his left hand and squeezed.

A thick, cloying perfume rose from the syrupy juice that ran out of the pulp and down his wrist. In the mashed mess in his palm there was suddenly a black worm crawling, a worm twice as long as his middle finger.

The barbarian flung the pulp and worm away. He wiped his hand on the lion hide, as if he'd touched something that was filthy beyond reckoning.

Another opening in the hedge admitted him to still one more boxed-in place, and for some time he went on like this through hedged rooms open to the soft, dully lighted sky.

He was beginning to grow frustrated, angry, when he heard voices.

The enchanted singing receded a little. Brak bellied down in the long black grass. He crept toward a dimly seen opening in the hedge. Through it the voices drifted.

Peering round, he saw an open place where the sward ran up a gentle hill. On its summit sat a white-pillared building much like a miniature temple. In the open interior, through which the breeze blew, a lamp flickered. On the shallow steps leading up to the structure stood the wizard Pom, Friar Hektor beside him.

Pom's huge hairless head gleamed in the perpetual twilight. As did his protruding eyes. He seemed composed, turning his head this way and that, slowly, to study his garden.

"I glanced away but a moment," Brak heard the wizard say. "When I looked back, she'd scuttled off."

"You'll never find her," Hektor told him. He sounded craven.

"Ah, you think not? Of course I will. This is my province. I know every nook of it. The girl hiding will make the game all the more tasty. In fact, I'm not certain but what I wanted her to flee, elude me for a while, just for the joy of the chase."

Slowly Pom turned to regard the Nestorian. The priest, Brak realized, was barely able to control his fright; he was shaking.

"That way"—Pom's voice whispered on the wind above the singing—"when I catch her and lay her bare on the sward, the taking will be all the more delicious." His odd, crookedly put-together body seemed to quiver faintly. He studied the garden.

Friar Hektor hesitated a moment. Then he plucked at Pom's poor robe.

The wizard spun to him, glaring.

"I'll help," the friar said.

"What do you mean?"

"I'll help search. I'll assist you in every way."

Pom pulled from the holy man's hand distastefully. His little mouth pursed up with cruel joy. "I thought you disciples of the Nameless God were strong, pure men."

"I am my own man. I"—Hektor licked his lips—"I want to live. How I got to this devil's place I don't know, but if I help you, I—I want a bargain. Return me to—wherever we came from. The real world. My life in return for my help." He clutched again. "Bargain, wizard?"

The bile of disgust climbed Brak's throat at the spectacle of the priest bargaining away his last shred of honor. But then, it wasn't so surprising, given Hektor's earlier behavior.

Pom brought his robe to his lips, as if to brush away a speck. He regarded the sky. Within the little white temple the lamp guttered in the wind.

"I will decide," Pom said.

Hektor swallowed, his throat-apple bobbing. "Not now? You won't tell me now?"

"No. You are a despicable man. I prefer a little amusement with you. I'll let you help in the hunt. Perhaps I'll even permit you to watch while the wench and I sport. Then I'll decide whether to return you, or kill you as I planned." Pom's wet eyes were amber and pink in the twilight. "Slowly, priest. Slowly, with exquisite hurt you cannot conceive until you experience it."

Friar Hektor backed down a step. "Madman. Madman."

Pom smiled. "Ah, indeed. But isn't it to be expected of a crippled bastard child cursed from birth? And remember, priest—this is my father's garden. In it you take my terms or you take none at all."

Hektor searched the hill, the sky, the hedges for a means of escape. There was none. His shoulders slumped pathetically. "I've no choice. Shall we search?"

Pom chuckled. "You're a filthy, reprehensible specimen indeed. But somehow I do enjoy you. Yes, we shall. First, though, I prefer to clean my hands and anoint myself so that I'm acceptable when we find her. Wait here."

So saying, the wizard turned and hitched his way up the steps. He vanished into the temple, a crippled wraith that seemed ready to topple over at any moment because of the outsized weight of its head.

Brak listened. Ever the distant singing. The coo-coo of a golden bird in a tree somewhere. But nary a sound to indicate where Shana might be hiding in terror.

The barbarian felt his own kind of fear, a controlled fear. Unless he was wary, he'd never locate her. How they would escape from this place he didn't know. But he put that greater problem away in order to solve the first: finding the girl.

Presently Pom reappeared from within the temple. He signed to Hektor and the two moved down the hill. They disappeared into an opening in the hedgerows to Brak's left.

The big barbarian took a firmer grip on the dagger, rose, and crept after them in a crouch.

He turned into the room of hedge into which they'd

vanished. It was very dark. He proceeded cautiously, unable to see the next opening. Somewhere he heard their footfalls. He moved in that direction.

He blundered into the tree without seeing it. Suddenly there was a flash of gold high up over his head against the sky. Disturbed, the metal bird spread its glittering wings. Its coo changed to a caw of rage.

Talons extended as it dropped down to Brak's face. The talons slashed.

Brak whipped his head aside in time to keep his eye from being put out. The talons scored a strike on his forehead, opening a wound that leaked blood into his eyebrows as the barbarian leaped back.

The roused bird circled, climbed, dived again, sharp golden beak driving for Brak's face.

He slashed his dagger hand up across from the right. The dagger point clanged harmlessly off the bird's wing. But the force of Brak's fist drove the bird aside. It seemed to flounder in the air a moment. Then its wings began beating strong again.

The bird shrilled and rilled, enraged. The noise carried. Pom exclaimed. There was much thrashing in the hedges.

Almost swifter than sight could follow, the bird shot up against the sky. Brak saw something that horrified him anew: a fat droplet oozing between the tips of the bird's upper and lower beak. A droplet secreted and hanging there—

A poison.

Poison for him.

Down streaked the bird, that black jewel glistening at the tip of the beak. Brak jumped two steps to the side. The bird wheeled and planed out level, coming for his face.

The knife was useless in Brak's hand. He jammed it

between his teeth, whipped up both hands and caught the bird's body. He stopped the beak but a hand's width in front of his face.

The bird beat its metal wings. Its talons raked Brak's hands bloody. The bird tried to wrench its head around to peck its poison drop into his thumb. But the barbarian held it off, his strength against its slippery, raking fury.

The beak quested around again, poking viciously. Brak slid his fingers up around the bird's neck, closed them there. He slid his other hand up to follow.

The bird drew its head back for a death-peck. Brak's temples beat with fear. He had but an instant—

Constricting both hands, he wrung the metal bird's neck. Twisted its head awry, tore it off—

Head separated from body. Golden wires hung between. There was a flash of whiteness, a billow of smoke, and Brak felt his face burned raw.

He shrieked like a wounded beast. Blinded, he flung the remains away. His entire face felt seared. The tangled wreckage of the bird dropped on the sward, glowing, molten, bubbling. The head with the glaring eye and the glistening drop in the beak dissolved into little liquid gold rivers that ran out through the black grass.

The knife fell from Brak's teeth. He made bestial sounds in his throat. His whole face was afire. As he stood there trying to press away the pain, there was a gurgling yell, and scrawny hands attacked his neck from behind.

A knee jolted the small of his back. Taken by surprise, he was driven forward. He crashed face first across the tiled coping of a pool.

The frantic, wordless panting of Friar Hektor became a bubbling roar in Brak's ears as the holy man,

with demented strength, thrust the barbarian's head under the water and held it there.

Silver danced in front of Brak's eyes. He tried to reach over his shoulder, grapple at the priest, but somehow the angle was wrong. The silver flakes before his eyes began to darken.

Water filled his nostrils, stung his burned face. Head completely submerged, he didn't dare breathe. His lungs began to pulse with pain.

Friar Hektor couldn't be all that strong. No, that was impossible. But then Brak knew otherwise: for the cowardly priest was bent on saving his own life by taking Brak's, and such men had the power of many.

Hektor's knee ground harder against his backbone. The barbarian's mind began to shimmer with a peculiar darkness. He knew he hadn't much longer to breathe, to live—

That thought gave him the will to fight the death-lethargy. He gathered all the power left in him, heaved upward—

Hektor fell off into the grass, caterwauling, *"Pom? Wizard? Where are you? Where have you gone? See, I've felled the outlander. Now you must help—!"*

Like one crazed, Brak went scrambling for the dagger he'd dropped. He knew approximately where it was, and he fought forward through the black grass, hands slashing and beating the sward. Friar Hektor was up. He leaped on Brak's back from behind.

Hektor's fingers dug into Brak's eye sockets. They pressed deep. Suddenly Brak touched metal. He closed his fist on the dagger hilt, aimed the point over his shoulder, hurled his fist up and back as Hektor's thumbs pressured his eyeballs into awful agony—

Friar Hektor choked. The sound was long and ugly. Then something warm splashed the barbarian's spine.

The pressure left his eyes. He crawled away, rolled over, squinted half blind—

Blood. That was blood on his back. It poured from the place where the knife had impaled Hektor's throat.

The Nestorian was stretched up on tiptoes. His hands were uplifted to the pink and amber sky. His face was awful to behold.

"Help me," he cried. *"Help me."*

No answer came from the god he'd forsaken; only the faraway voice of the woman singing of wicked pleasure. Gazing at perdition in the twilight clouds, Friar Hektor toppled forward. His fall jammed the dagger deeper into his neck. The point protruded from the back of his head, just below his fringe of hair.

A terrible wrath was upon Brak the barbarian. He lumbered over and kicked the Nestorian's twitching corpse so hard that it rolled to the pool and tumbled in. By the uncertain light Brak saw a dirty, skinny ankle sinking beneath the silvered surface. He raised his face to the sky and bayed like a victorious animal.

As the sound died away, he heard another—

Shana's scream.

Brak plunged his hands into the pool, seized the body, tore the dagger out of its throat by main force. Then he ran—crashed—through the hedge-rooms, back toward the open place from which the screaming rose.

His foot slipped as he emerged into the open area around the little white temple. On the shallow steps he saw Shana, fallen, Pom with her, spittle running from the corner of his mouth.

The girl's arms were scratched, and her legs as well. There was little left of her coarse skirt. Apparently Pom had torn it away. The wizard was bending over her, fighting her, pawing her blouse, ripping that too as he tried to lower his crippled body upon hers. All this Brak saw in an instant, just before he slipped, tumbled, hit the sward, and let out an inadvertent cry.

"One way or another, whore, one way or another, I'll have you," Pom was slathering, his hands everywhere on her. Then he heard Brak's thud and oath. The monstrous head swung around.

Pom's eyes loomed like gray moons. His delicate mouth convulsed.

Brak struggled to all fours. *Get up! Run! Use the knife!* his mind howled. But he was stunned by the fall and exhausted by his battle with the bird, by the burning of his face, by the pain in his eyes where Hektor had gouged. He slumped on the grass again. The dagger slipped out of his fingers.

Pom hitched down to the bottom step, leaving Shana next to naked. Her necklaces had been broken somehow. The green stones rained, *click-clack,* around her, an odd sound in contrast to the eerie, faraway singing.

Dazed, Brak once more tried to stand. Tried and could not. Pom seemed a study in unhurried motion, as if he understood that his adversary was weakened and doomed. His tiny child's hands rose upward, extended outward.

Brak knew in the depths of him that one bolt of crystal-white fire from those magical hands would destroy him. He was exposed, a target on the sward. Nowhere to hide and no strength to hide—

Pom's eyes glowed with maniacal fury. His delicate fingers wiggled ever so little, as if he were savoring the killing power that would flash from them.

Brak got to his knees, fumbled for a grip on the knife. Pom screamed some incoherent incantation, extended his arms full length. His fingertips lit with crystal brilliance—

Shana threw herself down the steps to attack him as the sound like a great bell pealed. She was a wild thing, hair flying, arms grappling Pom's legs at the instant the crystal-white fire leaped from his fingertips. Off-balance, he fell sideways.

Brak rolled frantically to avoid the bolt. But Pom's hands were flying up now, aimed at the pink and amber heavens. With a furious crackling, crystal-white fire raced for the clouds, trailing smoke, sizzling—

Dissipating.

On his feet, facing his last clean chance, Brak the barbarian flung his throwing hand back, then forward.

The dagger flew fast and true. Pom suddenly doubled over at the middle. He was painfully if not deeply wounded.

Pom tore at the handle sticking twisted into his threadbare robe. Brak could do no more this moment. He slumped down in total exhaustion, to let death come if it would.

Back in the hedges many golden metal birds began to shrill, as if sensing injury to their master. Pom sank to his knees, his huge, distended eyes growing ever more milky. *I haven't killed him,* Brak thought. *I have no more strength. But I haven't killed him.*

Shana's bare limbs gleamed. Pom toppled onto his side. The girl crawled on top of him, pried the dagger from his fingers and cut his throat.

Silence.

The faraway singing suddenly held a mournful note. All the metal birds stilled. Pom lay on his side on the white steps below the little temple where the lamp guttered in the wind. Blood poured out the mouth in his neck to blacken and dampen his robes.

Shana raised her head. Her face looked numb. Her hair hung in straggles. Just a few rags of blouse clung to her breasts.

Brak sucked air. Breathing hurt. Feebly he raised his hand to signal the girl that he was alive. As he lay on the sward, alive and vaguely grateful of that, he suddenly grew sick with a new despair.

They were trapped in an enchanted land, with no way of returning.

Presently he crawled to the girl. It was a journey of torment, but he made it. He held the girl's body in his arms. They huddled together, saying nothing, the only sounds their strident breathing.

Without warning the faces of two gods filled the sky above them.

8

Gods with the faces of evil men:

One was fat. Red-bearded. Moon-eyed and gaping. The other was scrawny, scrofulous, with a scar tracing upward from point of chin to left eye, then on across the ruins of an eyesocket that was no more than a mound of puckered white tissue.

The heads overloomed the garden. The mouths worked, as if the gods were speaking to one another. Shana looked long and hard for a moment. Then she went limp in Brak's arms.

He clenched his teeth against hysteria and stared up at the god-heads. Around them, as they filled half the sky, he saw strange, dark, pulsing spiked halos—shafts of grayness radiating from behind their heads. Within these shafts of halo danced things he half recognized. He was too numb, too hurt and fearful to fully understand the meaning of the specters and what he glimpsed around their heads.

The black sward began to undulate. Began to ripple gently, heave upward, sink down. The hedgerows began to quake and crack.

In an instant the rippling of the earth became more violent. The sky darkened. The spikes behind the heads of the gods grew long and large. The distant singing became minor key, harsh.

Hedges began to uproot. Great earthballs were torn loose as the land dropped away suddenly beneath them. Brak heard a fearsome cracking, turned—

The elegant white temple swayed, its pillars grinding at their foundations. Even as he watched, a long crack zigzagged upward through the heart of one of the pillars, then raced sideways in two directions to shear the pillar in half. The temple roof buckled.

Chunks of stone tore loose from it, falling to the interior. The lamp went out. Another pillar crumbled in great pieces. One came thundering down toward Brak and the unconscious girl.

He drove himself, harried himself until he found strength to drag her up across his shoulder and stagger down the shallow steps beginning to break apart beneath him. His foot nearly went into a crevasse that opened in the earth.

He reached the sward, barely able to stand because the earth was heaving up and down with terrible quakes. The pink and amber sky seemed to be collapsing, falling down upon them, and still the faces of the gods remained looming over all.

Peculiar faces, those, he thought in an almost dreamlike moment. Sullen and strangely witless. Coarse peasant faces—

Peasant faces.

The garden of Pom split apart, fissures racing in every direction. One opened under Brak's crotch, so that one foot was on either side.

He flung his weight leftward, teetered with both feet on the edge. Both hands on Shana's bare back, he wrenched himself violently hard, wrenched over and away from the gaping wound in the ground, from which foul odors arose. The hedgerows thrust up every which way, total carnage. The sky grew darker moment by moment. Back in their maze the golden metal birds beat their wings.

Brak's vision began to darken too. He knew full well that this might be the end of his life. Yet he also

knew that those strange, looming god-faces were a link to one last chance. If only he weren't so head-weary, so bone-weary! If only he could understand how and why he might save himself and the girl from the darkening holocaust of noise and shuddering earth—

The little temple collapsed upon itself, block crashing on block, pillar on pillar, total ruin.

Several sections rolled down and fell into the cracks in the earth and made no sound thereafter, as if the cracks had no bottoms. Brak breathed like a terrified animal, huddling with Shana in the middle of a patch of heaving sward, staring up dumbly at the two gods.

Peasant faces.

Darker grew the garden; darker. But in the spikes behind the heads of the gods Brak saw a smear of dull orange. As of fire. As of fire in—in a place he should recognize, if only he weren't so weary.

Shana moaned against his shoulder. Terror worked in her even though her mind was blanked by unconsciousness. Brak huddled and snarled and watched the chaos, the grinding, roaring destruction all around him. Time was all but gone.

*Peasant faces. Peasant faces staring down from—*where? At what?

PEASANT FACES—

And then, as the tiny cosmos of the garden wracked itself in noise and ruin, as the final moments of destruction roared up in a crescendo of grinding masonry, splitting earth, crashing foliage, Brak the barbarian laughed in a supreme madness. Surely what he understood, what he hoped, was just that—madness. Yet he knew no other way now. And madness was better than accepting this blind, furious death of crashing stone and gutted earth.

Struggling upright, he shot his hand high—*and touched the red beard of the god in the sky.*

Brak wound his fingers deep in the beard, and held on.

The god squealed.

The god tugged, pulled. Brak held on, held on, that one fist wound in long, tangly red hair—

Suddenly, Shana on his shoulder, he felt himself lifted.

He rose up from the heaving earth; up, away from the wracked garden, as if propelled or hauled by some magical force. Upward he rose, toward the faces of the gods.

Once he glanced down. The garden was growing smaller. He thought he saw the steps leading to the little temple break completely apart, and the corpse of Pom the wizard disappear down a long, endless fissure to the bottom of—where?

Everything blinked out.

9

The first thing Brak heard was a yowl of rage.

In other circumstances the sound might have had a certain comicality about it. He let go of a weight on his shoulder, heard something strike softly. Shana, falling—

Sick with nausea, he opened his eyes.

He found himself standing in the cottage of the woodsman, his hand tangled in the red beard of a god.

No, not a god. Just an immense, sinister-looking, moon-eyed man in rude clothes; a man who was cursing in a vile way even as he tried to pull away from Brak's hand.

Through swimming eyes Brak saw the cottage door standing open. Rain poured in. Behind him he heard the fire pop. He comprehended the orange light he had seen in the halos as he looked back from the garden of Pom to—here.

The other man held Pom's intricately stitched silk. It was torn in several places. The man had one strip of it tied around his forehead, an improvised bandana.

These were not gods but only woodland ruffians. The kind of men Shana had spoken about—

"Shana?"

He called her name wildly, found her lying at his feet, all but naked. He wiped his palm across his face. The skin hurt horribly, burned when the gold bird burst. The garden of Pom had heaved and shaken because—the barbarian did not understand *why*, only *how*—because these wandering looters had stolen upon the cottage and picked up the first and only item of apparent value: Pom's silk.

Why the woodsmen hadn't been propelled into the garden, he did not know. Perhaps because they had merely handled the silk instead of standing upon it. He was too tired to grapple fully with such an occult mystery, only knowing that by tugging the god's beard at the last instant had he somehow kept the link to reality unbroken, and pulled himself, and Shana, back from the neverland within the cloth—

The scrawny robber with one eye made the sign against evil and backed off, letting the torn silk fall. He clawed at a long curve-bladed knife stuck in his belt.

"Where do you come from?" he said through yellow stump teeth. "Where?"

"A naked gel—a wild man who just appears, pop!—they're demons!" exclaimed the other, moon-eyes red-beard. Brak wondered if he were going to faint. At any time the two would have been formidable adversaries. There was no hint of softness in them. He couldn't hope to fight them in his condition. All he could do was take advantage of their terror. Force himself to lean over, seize a leg of the overturned table. It used almost all his strength to break it off and brandish it—

But that was all that was needed. Shrieking, the two brigands fled from the cottage. A moment later their horses thundered away in the rain.

Half blind with pain, Brak bent, picked up the tatters of the silken garden of the wizard and flung them onto the embers on the hearth. Instantly foul black billows of smoke rolled forth.

The smoke filled Brak's mouth and stung his eyes. The stench was of the pit.

He shoved his hip against the broken table, tilted it, *crash,* half in and half out of the fireplace. He waited until the wood caught. Then he picked up Shana, and her precious carry bag, and his broadsword—cooled now—and stumbled from the cottage.

As he staggered down the weedy bank toward the foaming river, he heard a crackling behind. The cottage was beginning to burn.

He fell, slid, grabbed weeds to stop himself, crawled back up through the mud to the girl. He cradled her as best he could to protect her from the rain and cold and dark. Numb, he saw and heard nothing more.

10

The meadow was warm, the grasses waving and deep. Brak was a long while in kissing Shana one last time.

Finally they rose. Brak rearranged the lion hide about his middle. Behind them, smudgy with color on the horizon, was the rim of the woodland from which they had emerged after several days of journeying along the track. But they did not look that way. Rather they turned toward a crossroad marked with a signpost showing two directions.

The sun was high and hot, the meadow abuzz with insects as they left it and paused at the junction. In the distance, along the left-hand branching, men and women were haying a field. A dog yapped near a homestead. A rude cart driven by an old man approached from that direction.

Clad in clothing taken from the carry bag, the girl was combing her hair free of meadow grass. She looked quite lovely, Brak thought. With some reluctance he nodded at the right fork of the road.

"That's my way to the south, you say?"

"Aye, Brak. The other way's to Thenngil, and my cousin's farm." She touched him. "I'll not ask to go with you, because you're not a man to travel with another for long."

"And I'll not ask you to go, because then I might not."

Awkwardly he bent and cupped her chin and kissed her. He looked long into her eyes, remembering the heat of their morning in the meadow and their nights huddled under blankets back along the track in the gloomy wood, from which, it had seemed several times, they might never emerge.

"Say this for the crazed wizard," remarked Brak with a tenderness that surprised him. "He had an eye for a fair face."

She leaned up to give him another kiss. He knew a pang of regret, a moment's hesitation. Then the song of Khurdisan began to sing in his ears, like a woman's song, but more sweetly than that which he had heard in Pom's unclean garden.

The old fellow driving the cart reached the junction. He gave them an unfriendly stare as he went by. Shana smiled. It did no good. So Brak scowled. That sent the old duffer on his way hastily.

Shana picked up her carry bag and began to walk along the left-hand road. She waved once, then went on. Her step was sure, her head high, her deep red hair bright in the sunshine. Good. The memories might not be too somber, then. She might dream nightmares of the garden-in-the-cloth, but perhaps she would kiss someone again sometime, and laugh, and even bear strong sons. Good.

His pony had been gone when he woke on the riverbank that morning to find the woodsman's cottage reduced to smoking rubble. But he didn't mind walking. The sun felt fine on his naked shoulders, and the soothing paste Shana had put on his seared cheeks and the clawed places on his forehead had begun to heal the skin.

He whistled a low, tuneless melody. His yellow braid and the lion tail bobbed in rhythm. He flung his broadsword up across his huge shoulder, point backward, and as he marched south the metal caught the sun and flashed.

THE GIRL IN THE GEM

The yellow-headed barbarian had been sleeping but a short and fitful time when the sinister troop of dwarfs stole down upon him.

The shutters of the inn's large window creaked open. A bulbous, misshapen head stood out against the stars in the opening. Another appeared, a third.

Faint monkeylike footfalls scurried over the roof tiles. A half dozen little bodies leaped from the roof to the yard outside the window, a half dozen more, until the starry night sky seemed to rain tiny figures. Dwarf hands clasped the sill. Then, with a batlike belling of a silken cloak, the first of them was inside.

Lonesome and weary after riding many days down through the hills to the port beside the purple-foamed sea, Brak the barbarian had feasted heavily at the empty inn. He'd squandered his last few dinshas for wine, and the wine had taken its toll. He sprawled full length atop a trestle table now, stirring and muttering in haunted sleep as, on tiny feet, the dwarfs came jumping through the window and scurrying through the stealthily opened door.

Brak's brawny arms and single long yellow braid hung down off the table. Just below his outstretched fingers an empty wine goblet lay on its side. His gigantic chest heaved up and down as he breathed raggedly. He was wide-shouldered and naked save for a garment of lion's hide about his hips. A great broadsword scabbard gleamed beside his mighty leg.

The dwarfs gathered about the table like mourners

at a bier. The leader of the group leaned down. He grasped the fallen wine goblet. With a little leap he hurled it up against the rafters.

"He wakes," the leader squeaked. "Knives out!"

The wine cup fell back to the floor, clanking. Brak sat up. He rubbed his eyes. Then pit-fear, cold and harrowing, clutched his bowels.

The dwarfs caught the table edge and used it to vault up. With a great roar of rage Brak tried to throw off the little cloaked figure landing hard on his chest. By the starglare coming through the window, he saw a flicker of silver-white metal. Wildly he twisted his head to the side. A knife in a tiny fist chunked into the wood next to his ear.

More of the dwarfs swarmed upon him. Brak gathered his strength, gave one huge heave. Tiny bodies flew.

Brak leaped off the trestle table. All around his legs the air whispered as dwarf hands whipped knives back and forth. He slid the mighty broadsword free of its sheath, raised it over his head with both hands on the haft.

Then something stayed him. The dwarfs chittered softly, screeched unintelligibly.

But not once did a blade point prick his skin. It was as though they deliberately intended to miss.

"Stand away!" Brak bellowed. "I warn you—stand away or I'll hack you up."

This shout was the big barbarian's concession to the guilt he suddenly felt at the prospect of having to bring the broadsword down upon men so much smaller than he. It seemed unfair, almost. The dwarfs screeched devilishly, and their brandished daggers still flashed. But no steel touched his skin.

Brak wondered whether he was still asleep and imprisoned in a nightmare. "The window!" one of the dwarfs chirruped.

He pivoted on a miniature heel, vaulted up into the shutter frame, crook-backed against the stars.

"Leave him!"

And, like insects or plague rats, the dwarfs began an exodus as swift as their arrival.

Rubbing his eyes, Brak rushed to the door, then into the yard. Already the dwarf company, a dozen, two dozen, was up away over the roof tiles, to vanish down the other side. The inn building backed against a high wall overlooking a sour street. Out there Brak heard footfalls die away.

His pony tethered in the yard's corner stamped and blew. "A light," Brak muttered. "Where in the name of Shaitan is a lanthorn?"

He blundered noisily back inside the inn. From abovestairs a voice cried, "What's going on down there? Must you make all that racket, outlander?"

"Haul yourself off your pallet, landlord, and come down here," Brak shouted.

He located a dark lantern beside a great hogshead resting on logs. By the time he had struck sparks and blown the lantern alight, the oafish, porcine landlord in his night-robe appeared.

"I heard a commotion," the landlord said testily. "More looters? Aye, we've had nothing but riot and rapine in the streets for a fortnight, ever since the earth shook and Great Tyros rose from beneath the waves again offshore." The landlord bent over. "What mice tracks are these?" He pointed to the traces of tiny footprints left on the dirt floor.

"A pack of little assassins swarmed in on me," Brak said. "Why, the gods only know."

"Little assassins?"

"Dwarf men."

The landlord turned red. "You're still drunk. Swallow your tongue for blasphemy."

Not understanding the remark, Brak growled, " 'Tis true. There was a pack of them, carrying knives they somehow did not want to use." Quickly Brak told the tale.

The landlord's face showed mixed horror and revulsion. "Do you want to be hung up by your heels? Keep that drunken vision to yourself, or you'll wish you'd never ridden into this city."

Now Brak was growing angry. "Do you deny the evidence of those tracks?"

The landlord gazed at the rafters. "I see nothing, stranger."

"In the name of all the devils—!" Brak shouted, rushing forward to seize the man.

The landlord darted back, bawled, "Outlander, there are no dwarfs in the port kingdom of Lesser Tyros save those tiny men who wear the livery of the king, Archimed of the Wide Sails, the very lord who lies ill with the fatal fever in the palace. Already the black crepes are hung from monuments and eaves in preparation for his passing. When disaster and mourning have already fallen upon us, surely you dare not accuse the king's own retainers of prowling the dark to loot."

"The little men are in—your ruler's service?" Brak said, astonished.

"Aye. I repeat, there are no others in Lesser Tyros. Therefore you'd be wise to say you saw nothing, no matter what you saw."

"Be damned! I saw a troop of tiny devils who—"

"You saw *nothing*, if you wish to live for other sunsets," repeated the landlord and hurried back to his chambers above the inn room.

Angrily Brak slammed his broadsword back into the scabbard. He stalked outside into the waning starlight.

This cursed kingdom was afflicted with more assorted madnesses than he'd ever encountered anywhere else during his long journey down from the high steppes, the wild lands of the north where he'd been born. Bound to seek his fortune in the warm climes of Khurdisan far southward, Brak had let his pony's hoofs lead him through ragged foothills to the dilapidated port named Lesser Tyros.

Days ago, while he was still riding up in those same hills, Brak had felt the very earth tremble. He'd seen rockslides crashing off the peaks. Upon arriving in Lesser Tyros and taking space at the deserted inn, he had been told that the area roundabout had been struck by one of the infrequent earth-shakings which, in years past, had caused the original city of Great Tyros to sink beneath the waves of the purple-foamed sea. This latest cataclysm had retwisted the sea bottom somehow. As a result a collection of gleaming green-and-purple spires and buildings now thrust upward in plain sight above the water offshore. Brak himself had seen the slime-festooned towers at sundown, from the top of one of the hills upon which Lesser Tyros was built.

The portion of Great Tyros, home of sea-kings and merchant-adventurers, so the landlord said, had simply reappeared a fortnight ago when the earth trembled. A part of an equally long-sunken causeway leading out to the ruins had also become visible again. The natural disaster had triggered a flood of nocturnal lootings and, as a cap to all the other woes of the area, the ruler, Archimed of the Wide Sails, had been stricken ill by the kingly plague a few days later. Palace seers foresaw his death quite soon.

Pondering all these strange circumstances, Brak did not for a moment hear the jingle of traces and clatter of armor in the street outside the wall. As he glanced up, the gates were thrust open. Officers wearing breastplates of beaten brass and carrying pikes and lanterns swarmed through the yard.

Several rushed inside the inn, reappeared carrying a coarse clothwork bag which they immediately opened.

"Here, commander," a soldier called. " 'Twas carelessly hid under the trestle table." A fist dug into the bag, and drew out a platter which gleamed gold. Then came a gem-studded cup and another platter.

Dim suspicions whirled in Brak's head. He dropped his hand to his broadsword. The commander of the force turned, came stalking back, pointed at him.

"Hold that one. From the looks of him, he's a foreigner. He did not even bother to hide his spoil."

Quickly a ring of pikes formed, sharp and gleaming, around the barbarian. The commander approached closer.

"Tonight the palace storehouses were desecrated by a thief," he said. "And it now appears we have found that thief. Better you'd taken your loot and ridden out, you simpleton. Because now you face punishment. Take his arms and bring him along!"

The mission of the dwarf pack made a kind of warped sense at last. "This is mummery!" Brak shouted. "That sack is none of mine. It was planted there by a flock of little men who—"

"Shut the liar's mouth and fetch him," the commander cut in. A pike butt slammed Brak in the side of the head.

Snarling, the big barbarian reeled back. He whipped out his broadsword. His face was savage. The single long yellow braid of his hair swung back and forth as he crouched to fight.

A soldier darted in from the left. Brak understood now why the dwarfs had not attacked. That was not their mission. Rage and fury reddened his mind as he thrust his right arm out, the broadsword point racing for the charging soldier's throat.

Against the back of his skull a pike butt hammered. Another, another, another.

Its killing stroke undelivered, the broadsword dropped from Brak's hand. He spun, cursing, flailing. There were too many of them. He keeled over.

Brak was trussed with cording. He was thrown across the back of a horse. From this undignified and painful position he saw the commander of the soldier troop pass a purse to the oafish landlord. The latter had appeared in the shadows of the inn door and smiled smugly.

So that was how it was done, Brak thought grimly as the troop started through the dark, hilly streets, hoofs clattering, torches flaring. The innkeeper kept a lookout for a likely victim and then sent word to the palace.

But why did the palace need a victim at all?

And what kind of kings ruled Lesser Tyros that they should resort to such trickery?

Brak did not know. He only knew that his trouble was dire, and his broadsword gone.

As the horses clopped along the hilly streets, Brak several times glimpsed the newly risen spires of Great Tyros gleaming far out at the end of the half-sunken causeway. Presently palace walls shut out the view.

The palace of Lesser Tyros was a huge collection of stone buildings fronting on the harbor which was filled with rotting, sagging merchant galleys that gave testimony to the kingdom's declining maritime status. Brak was carried in through a huge courtyard where mourning banners already fluttered. He was dumped unceremoniously on his feet in a vast, high-vaulted hall. Beyond its windows the spires of Great Tyros were visible again, glowing eerily in the starshine.

The soldiers unfastened the cording. Brak stood in a docile manner, determined to await developments. A gong beat somewhere. The soldiers retreated. Huge doors closed. The shrill soprano keening of female mourners rose up in a ritual song, echoing as though the music sounded and resounded through many corridors.

From behind a filigreed screen a girl appeared. She was fragile as porcelain, alone and unarmed.

But she walked with head held high. Her gown was cut of the rich purple cloth of Tyros which Brak had seen in marketplaces far away. Upon her black-raven hair was a circlet of gold decorated with peculiar zodiacal symbols. She was young, full-bodied, imperious, with wave-green eyes. She glanced at Brak's shoulders, the savage cast of his features, his long braid, his lion-hide garment. She smiled with her berry-red lips.

"Have they given you back your sword?"

"Given me—?" Brak gaped. "No, lady. If they do, I'll cut a throat or two, I vow."

The girl laughed. She settled on a divan, indicated a tall amphora. "Please. Drink some wine to calm your rage. We had no choice but to send the palace dwarfs to plant a sack of household plate and thus cause you to be arrested as a criminal. But there is no need for us to quarrel now, or grow ugly with one another, so long

as you fully understand your situation. For, you see, the crime of which you're accused is punishable by heel-hanging, your head over live coals, until you simmer or strangle to death. Yet there is another way. Please. Have some wine."

On the point of erupting with anger, Brak laughed. The wench had a certain audacity.

He stalked over, picked up the amphora, drank without bothering with goblets. He swiped his forearm across his mouth. "My name is Brak. As long as you've arranged my fate so neatly, at least do me the honor of telling me yours."

"Marjana," she said. "It is my father Archimed of the Wide Sails who lies dying. I will succeed him when his illness has run its course."

"You—" Brak gestured. "—will rule this kingdom?"

"Presently, yes. For that task, I need help. The help of my younger sister. One woman cannot begin to control this unruly realm of rogues and sea-rovers. That is why I must send you where no man of this household has courage to go—or, indeed, I fear, the strength. You must go to the Sea-Stone. You must bring back my younger sister Mardela, if truly she still lives, so that she may sit beside me and help me rule."

Brak scowled. "What is this Sea-Stone of which you speak?"

"A great gem blue as the deeps. It once burned in a place of honor above the throne of my father's grandsires, the kings who ruled Great Tyros."

"Where is this fabulous stone?"

Slowly Marjana raised her hand. Gracefully she pointed.

"Out there."

Brak followed the tip of her finger. His brows knotted together. For she had indicated one of the open window embrasures high above the dilapidated hulls in the harbor, and she was pointing to the beslimed, strangely phosphorescent towers of Great Tyros that rose from beneath the purplish lapping waves.

Before Brak could speak, Marjána continued:

"When I was younger, there was a warlock in my father's court who intrigued behind his back. When my father discovered this, he ordered him punished. Executed. Before this could happen, the warlock burned sacred powders and drew diagrams upon the floor of his apartment. My younger sister Mardela vanished. Before he died under excruciating torture, the warlock said he had imprisoned Mardela in endless sleep within the Sea-Stone, in the palace of Great Tyros which had long before sunk beneath the waves.

"Only a fortnight ago, as you've doubtless heard, the land in these parts heaved and shook again. The chronicles say such a cataclysm sank Great Tyros long ago. Now the towers thrust up once more. Or a part of them, anyway. So if Mardela is truly imprisoned within the Sea-Stone out there, neither living nor dead these many years, it requires but the hack of a great sword to smash the stone and loose her."

"Send your own men," Brak snarled.

She shook her head. "Great Tyros is a haunted place. Even offered fabulous rewards, or faced with threats of death, the soldiers will not go. We have been searching for a strong man who would. It can be no more than an hour's journey, out and back. If Mardela is not within the stone—if the warlock lied—no harm is done. But if she sleeps in the gem—she did indeed vanish completely when the warlock cast his spell—then I want her beside me, to help me rule when my father breathes his last. If you will go, I will pay a purse of one hundred dinshas. If you refuse, then the punishment for the crime of which you are accused will be carried out before the sun has set again."

Brak gnawed his lip, rumbled, "I should be flattered by your faith in me. I do not think I am."

Marjana shrugged. "Be that as it may, the choice is clear." For an instant her eyes flickered with a warmth that set Brak's backbone tingling. "And I can offer other rewards, Brak."

"That is evident." He paused. "Very well. I will strike the bargain."

Now Marjana smiled a little, her lips shining in the torch flare. "So quickly decided?"

Brak shrugged. "My purse is empty. A hundred dinshas will speed me nicely on my way to the lands of Khurdisan to the south if I succeed. Should I refuse you, then I will never know what fortune has stored up for me over the horizon, now will I?"

"That is true. You will die heel-hung, a common criminal."

"At least your forcing is in the open."

Now Marjana rose, crossed to him in a swirl of purple garments. "I will be more than kind to you when you return, barbarian, as I would be more than cruel if you refused. I loved my younger sister dearly. If it can be done, I wish to have her restored to me."

Suppressing a certain grudging admiration for the girl's strength, Brak said, "Give me an ample meal, and wine, and a few hours rest. It has been a long night, Princess Marjana, full of twists and turns."

Marjana reached up, touched his cheek. "There is yet another peril."

"Surely not, after so many already unveiled."

"The Hellarms," she said.

Unaccountably Brak's spine crawled. "What are they?"

"A myth, perhaps, but fisherfolk maintain they have seen them—or it. A great black beast with many arms like whips. It swims among the sunken towers. It is said to be ten times bigger than a man." Mockingly she added, "Are you afraid?"

The Hellarms. The name rang in Brak's brain like some sinister chord. *The Hellarms.*

"I would be a fool not to be. But I have faced the demons of this world before."

"Then take this." Marjana drew from her girdle a scarf of a particularly dark wine-colored silk, marbled and mottled, with a tiny stain of white at one corner. "My own scarlet scarf, as a token of my wish for your success." And she tied the silk around the bosses of his empty broadsword scabbard.

Then she rose on tiptoes to press his mouth warmly, even wantonly, with hers.

Holding her by the shoulders, Brak chuckled. He did not really know whether to damn her for a conniving sly fox or admire her for her frank use of her power. Rulers were a strange breed. And certainly the world through which he traveled was full of strange rulers of every stamp. If she wanted her younger sister returned, and would pay a hundred dinshas, he was a fool not to try, especially considering the alternative.

As Marjana summoned her dwarfs with a clap of her hands, Brak found his gaze drawn out the window to the slimed spires beginning to gleam brighter in false dawn. Was it all a sea-sunken dream, the Sea-Stone where the younger princess was prisoned and the Hellarms floating in the deep? He would learn soon enough.

"This way, this way, mighty lord," one of the dwarfs chittered, ushering Brak out. Shaking his head in puzzlement, the big barbarian went loping away to one of the palace apartments.

At moonrise the next night Marjana and two of her dwarfs led Brak down and down through labyrinthine passages to a nail-studded door deep within the palace. Swung inward, the door revealed the purple-brackish water of the harbor a short distance below. A punt bumped against the foundation stones.

Without a word Brak accepted his broadsword from one of the dwarfs.

"Come back safely with Mardela, and the sword will never leave your side again," Marjana called as Brak clambered down into the punt. He undid the painter and used the pole to push off.

Lights gleamed in the towers of Lesser Tyros on the mainland. But the spires of Great Tyros lying beyond the rotting hulls among which Brak poled were dark. The night wind was piercing, the sea a wide curving gleam of silver-darkness. The air smelled of salt spray.

Brak stood in the punt with his great legs braced apart, poling vigorously. From his scabbard fluttered Marjana's wine-hued scarf. Presently he left the last of the anchored merchantmen behind. The punt moved onto the empty waters toward the rerisen causeway whose sheared-off end reared ahead.

The nearer Brak approached, the taller loomed the intricately fluted spires of the cluster of buildings thrust up from the sea. The punt bumped against the crumbled causeway. Brak tied up, wedging the painter in a crack in one of the causeway blocks. He clambered up on the slippery stones, stared ahead.

Far at the causeway's end a huge, black arch yawned. Carrying a length of resinous wood in one hand, the other hand on his broadsword haft, Brak loped toward it, a tiny figure beneath the shadowed immensity of the towers festooned with great green loops of sea fungus. The closer Brak came to the buildings, the stronger grew the stench of weedy wetness.

As he drew near the looming arch, Brak paused. He struck sparks, finally got the torch going in the gusty air. The wind whined, sang, keened as he stepped through the arch, which was actually an opening in what must have once been a city wall.

He walked across a wide, squarelike space paved with gigantic marble blocks butted together crookedly and tilted at odd angles. Some of the blocks had crumbled away altogether. In these openings the purplish water rose up, forming pools. Brak suspected that a vast network of underwater canals ran below the shaky structures towering to the moon.

Ahead a mammoth, imposing, and many turreted edifice rose. Broad steps led up to its entrance. Just as Brak was climbing these steps, a strange, flitting radiance caught his attention.

He whirled. The light winked and vanished, down in one of the pools left by missing paving stones.

Brak's flesh crawled. For one dreadful instant he had imagined that, down in the pool, a great yellow-blotchy eye of inhuman size had looked up at him.

Brak stopped at the top of the steps, cursed low. The wind, soughing around building corners, had blown out his torch. He struggled to kindle fresh sparks. The air was too damp. Swallowing, he cast the half-burned wood aside. He snaked out his broadsword with a faint whisper of iron on iron.

He passed between two great pillars, blinked. Ahead there was a faint pearl-blue glow. Careful of each step, Brak moved into the palace of blackness toward that narrow, vertical, flamelike blueness.

Abruptly he banged against damp, sea-cold metal. He had blundered into great doors, he discovered. The bluish radiance washed through the narrow vertical opening between them. Brak slid his sword away, braced his palms on the doors, thrust. He gasped with exertion. The doors, ponderous metal, gave but little.

He bent his back. The huge muscles in his shoulders writhed and corded. All at once the right-hand door gave all the way. Brak stumbled forward into a burst of blue light.

He caught himself just in time to keep from falling over a stone lip into water below.

Panting from exertion, Brak raised his head. He was in a gigantic chamber whose walls were decorated with fantastically colored friezes depicting the mighty vessels of the sailor-kings of Great Tyros. The pool below, in which Brak's image rippled and reflected blue, was in actuality the all-but-disintegrated sunken central floor of a throne room. Only a few paving blocks could be glimpsed down in the purplish depths. The bluish radiance hurt Brak's eyes. Despite this he raised his head. He goggled at the sight on the far side of the chamber.

A massive golden carved throne chair sat tilted on a cocked block of flooring. Above it, embedded in the stone wall and five times as high as Brak was tall, shone the Sea-Stone.

It was an immense transparent gem of a thousand or more facets, deep and cool-blue as a peaceful ocean. And within it was a human figure. The figure of a young girl without clothing, perfectly preserved.

Her head was bowed forward as though she slept. Her hands were folded over the lower part of her body, thereby also concealing her bosom. Her hair was white as silver as she hung in the crystalline-blue prison high over Brak's head.

"True, then," he whispered. "Mardela in the Sea-Stone."

He felt encouraged, even though the girl whose hair must have turned white looked lifeless behind her blue-walled catacomb. Quickly Brak surveyed the chamber.

He could not cross the sunken floor because it did not exist. But he could make his way around the chamber on the narrow rim on which he now stood. He wanted to make quick work of the job if possible. The shadows in the chamber, coupled with the gem's blue light which must have shone for centuries in unearthly radiance under the sea, somehow unnerved him.

Being careful of his footing, he began to pad around the stone rim of the chamber. Halfway down the long side, he started. He whipped his head to the right.

The surface of the water in the center of the chamber rippled, boiled, erupted with a string of bubbles. Deep, deep below, there was a yellow flash, swiftly gone.

Brak yanked out his sword. He raced around toward the crazy-tilted throne chair. Had he seen the Hell-arms? Was it the same eye which had watched him outside the once-sunken city? Were there passages between the foundations through which a—*thing*—could swim and await the coming of its prey?

Still as death the white-haired girl hung up there inside the gem. Brak calculated swiftly. He climbed up on the arms of the golden throne. The gem's radiance was so bright it nearly blinded him. He closed both hands on the broadsword hilt. Reaching high, he uttered a silent, terse prayer to the unknown gods and

brought the broadsword blade whistling forward with all the power of his mighty body.

The impact nearly knocked him from his perch. Thinking he had failed, he drew his sword back for another blow. Suddenly a star-shaped crack appeared in a lower facet of the gem.

Like a spiderwebbing of ice, the crack shot outward, became many cracks, and, with a thunderous smash and clatter, the Sea-Stone fell into great sharp pieces that rained down.

Brak instinctively ducked his head. He was battered off the chair by one of the huge fragments whose sharp edge ripped open his left shoulder. A moment later he lay on his back, blood sliming his biceps, dazed.

He lurched up. Fear quickened his breathing. The mammoth oval in the wall into which the Sea-Stone had been set was empty. Wind whistled through it. All around, like a meadow of crystal, great cruel-cornered bits of the Sea-Stone gleamed. Each fragment radiated blue light. The throne chamber had become a patchwork of intersecting, dazzling beams and glitters.

Brak stumbled forward, cut his ankle on a shard lying in his path. Another big piece teetering on the stone ledge fell off, plopped, and sank into the chamber's watery center. Behind still another fallen section of the gem, a section as wide as Brak was tall, a strand of silver hair lay damply.

Certain the fall had killed her if she was not already dead, Brak rushed around the piece of stone. He choked back an exclamation of surprise.

The girl Mardela lay on her side, her silver hair around her like a shimmering garment. A bit of the stone had cut into her calf. From the short, shallow wound, red blood trickled.

Brak reached over, touched the girl's shoulder. She moaned lightly. Brak pressed his lips to her cheek, felt the flesh warming beneath the touch of his mouth. She had slumbered within the Sea-Stone, imprisoned there by the warlock's spell, but she had not died.

Brak turned her over gently, to pick her up and carry her from the chamber and the ruins of Great Tyros. Doing so, he saw her face clearly for the first time.

Tiny wrinkles radiated from the corners of Mardela's closed, porcelain-lidded eyes. She was not an old woman, but neither was she a young maiden. Brak scowled, grunted under his breath. The stink of treachery was in his nostrils.

Something black, thick, jellyish, as round as his own huge torso, curled around Brak's leg where he crouched. Glancing down, Brak cried out.

A pinkish, suckerlike orifice as wide as his arm was long gleamed and pulsed on the undersurface of the black thing which now began to wrap itself round and round his leg.

The orifice touched his flesh. Brak threw his head back, shrieked in mortal agony as the sucker began to strip the skin from his leg.

Maniacally Brak hauled his broadsword back. He chopped it downward behind him. There was a sudden noise of erupting, churning water. As his blade cleft the tentacle, the orifice against his leg relaxed. Brak fought free of the slimy black tube twisted around him, staggered to his feet—

As the Hellarms rose from its underwater lair.

Brak's mind threatened to crack at the sight of the monster that came plowing and heaving up from the endless fathoms below the ancient city. The center of its body was a huge, black, obscenely shimmering pulplike dome nearly ten times as high as Brak himself. This central dome swayed higher and higher, rising toward the distant ceiling while tentacle after mammoth tentacle emerged from the water, came slithering over the rim of the stone on which Brak stood. Two immense baleful yellow-blotchy eyes, pupilless, flamed in the dome.

The Hellarms seemed to have scores of the whiplike tentacles. One went streaking for Brak's scabbard, swaying in the air just a hand's width from the place where Marjana's wine-colored scarf was knotted. The orifice of the tentacle opened and closed and emitted whistling, sucking noises with an insane frequency not matched by the orifices of the other tentacles which came slithering and crawling toward Brak, to surround him and strip off his skin.

Horror-struck, Brak hacked out at the first tentacle, split it. A gush of foul-smelling tarry liquid spilled over the stones. Another tentacle sailed at his head, whipped past as Brak dodged backward. He slammed against a big fragment of the Sea-Stone. His spine was cruelly cut by one of its sharp edges.

The attacking tentacles swept over Brak's head. The end curled back toward the lower center of the dome in which yawned a huge, rotting-pink mouth opening. But the tentacle had no human gobbet to drop into the central mouth, which closed suddenly. All at once the orifices in the tentacles began to whistle and make sucking sounds at a faster rate, as though the monster were angered.

Still the tentacles swaying near Brak's scabbard did not fasten. It wavered back and forth near the knotted scarf and, through his pain and fright, Brak at last understood why Marjana had given him the bit of silk.

The deep-hued dye was a human dye which drew the Hellarms. It was blood.

He cursed himself for a fool for not guessing it. The marbled swirls of the color should have made it apparent, and also the whitish corner, which was not a stain, but a place where the blood had not seeped and colored.

It was too late for such self-cursing. Brak had trouble enough staying on his feet, hacking madly at this tentacle, then that one. The Hellarms thrashed and writhed and threw up fountaining sprays of water in the sunken center of the chamber. All at once one of the tentacles caught Brak off guard and wrapped round and round his middle.

He was blinded by blood from his wound, by spray from the pool. He felt the orifice close on his belly, sending hot agonies of pain through his body.

Other tentacles swiped at his head, missed, went curling and sailing back in dumb instinctual response toward the central mouth of the dome. Wildly Brak sliced and hacked at the tentacle around his waist. He sawed back and forth, back and forth, until the blackish fibrous stuff parted, spilling out more of the tarry effluvium.

He peeled the severed end away from his belly, leaped back shaking with pain as the orifice came free. Panting, he stumbled backward, crouched above the unconscious Princess Mardela while the angered whistlings and sucking of the Hellarms increased, denoting its maddened frustration.

Six tentacles came crawling over the rim of the stone ledge, all sliding toward Brak's body at once. He raised his sword, then lowered it. He sobbed raggedly. To struggle with a puny iron blade was futile. He could not win against the creature.

Long yellow braid dappled with blood and hanging

over his shoulder, Brak leaned his head against the cool blue-radiating surface of a gigantic fragment of the Sea-Stone. He gulped air. The tentacles came crawling, slithering, creeping toward his legs—

In the corner of his vision the bluish radiance of the great chip of Sea-Stone burned. Wildly Brak slammed his broadsword back in the scabbard. He darted behind the huge fragment, which was precariously balanced upon one of its shatter-cut facets. He leaned his shoulder against the hunk of stone which towered twice his height.

Thrusting and bending his huge back, cursing aloud and calling on the nameless gods, he tipped the great chip over with a crash. The tumbling, glittering-blue glasslike piece smashed down atop the out-creeping tentacles.

Instinctively the tentacle orifices closed. The tentacle ends turned—and while Brak watched, the six obscenely black tubes together lifted the mighty chunk of Sea-Stone, carried it out high in the air to the central dome, and rammed it into the pink-rotting mouth.

The mouth closed.

Then, as the knife-sharp edges of the fragment cut and sliced away at the inside of the monster's maw, new horror began.

Swallowing the instrument of its own destruction, the Hellarms began to writhe, crash about the pool even more wildly. Poisonous ichor gushed from its suddenly opened mouth, deep inside which the fragment of Sea-Stone was now lodged, choking and cutting, choking and cutting—

The tentacles one by one slid thrashing back into the pool. The baleful yellow eyes began to pulse and dim, pulse and dim. With its whistling rising higher and higher, until Brak's ears began to ache and throb, the Hellarms sank downward into water darkening with the tarry ichor.

Groggy, hurt, Brak felt dimly that the Hellarms *knew* a human being had slain it with a jagged gem which cut its insides to bits. He felt the Hellarms knew because the baleful yellow eyes pulsed flame-bright an instant before the monster sank.

One last tentacle reached feebly over the rim of the ledge. Brak hacked it off. The Hellarms vanished from sight, yellow eyes dwindling and dwindling—

Hardly remembering the rest of it, Brak the barbarian gathered the still-living Mardela in his arms. He trudged around the rim of the sunken floor. He walked out of the palace and under the arch. Mardela's hair hung silver-damp in the starlight. Brak's eyes were wet with mixed sweat and blood. For a moment he did not glimpse what was waiting for him at the crumbled end of the causeway.

Off to the right, out below the foaming purple waves, there was a will-o'-the-wisp flicker of yellow, now bright, now dull. But Brak's gaze fastened straight ahead.

A second punt was tied beside the one he had poled.

A figure stood on the causeway.

A cloak belled from its shoulders, rippled by the wind which blew from behind Brak now. The figure held a bow, fully drawn. The arrowhead shone in the glare of the waning moon.

Suddenly a gust of wind blew back the cowl. Marjana's hair streamed out in the wind.

"No one told me that she was your younger sister," Brak shouted. "No one except you."

"Stand there, barbarian," Marjana cried. "This arrow can travel faster than your legs."

"She's alive," Brak called back, taking a pace forward. His eyes were fastened on that trembling arrow tip standing far out ahead of the bow's curve. "Alive, and not a young girl, either. Your *older* sister. And therefore heiress to the crown of King Archimed, am I right?"

"As long as she was prisoned in there—" Marjana screamed, "—she was—threat—" The wind blew away some of her words as Brak took another pace forward, another. "—if it turned out—she was alive—someday, someone might—free her—"

"So you cleverly trapped me as a criminal and set me to learn whether she did truly live," Brak responded in a ragged shout. "Of course you could send no one from your household, because they would have smelled a plot. The dwarfs, for instance. They might not complain at hoodwinking an outlander on the request of their mistress, but to slay a rightful holder of the throne—? I doubt their loyalty to you would go that far. So you gave me a token of your faith when you sent me. A scarf. A dyed scarf. Dyed with blood. Dyed with the blood whose silent tang you knew the Hellarms would somehow recognize, somehow scent. With that scarf you gave me the very means by which I'd be slain, and your sister too."

Now, far on his right, Brak noticed a pulsing yellow flash, bright, then dark. He knew then that there must indeed be subterranean canals beneath the thrust-up ruins of Great Tyros. Through them the Hellarms had come lumbering along in the depths, maddened, death-wounded, but chasing to the last its slayer.

Brak heard a ripple of water, a foaming roar. Something slapped and sucked wetly and came slipping across the causeway.

"No further!" Marjana screamed, drawing the bow

to full nock. "I can kill you before you half reach me. Barbarian, stop! Stop, I'll—"

Shrieking, she released the arrow. Brak had bent swiftly, dropping Mardela. Running forward, he did not lurch out of the way in time. The arrow plowed through his left thigh. It left a deep, bloody gorge into which the blood from his hacked left arm drained and mingled. But the fingers of his right hand were busy ripping at silk.

He raised his hand. Something fluttered, whipped by the wind. It skated through the air the short distance to Marjana's head, fluttered there, held against her face by the wind blowing from behind Brak.

Too late she recognized what it was, flung away her bow, plucked madly at it—

Just as two slimed-black tentacles of the dying Hellarms slithered along the causeway, scented the silent tang of the blood-dyed scarf, wrapped around Marjana's body.

High against the waning moon she was lifted, shrieking, dying. One of the ghastly orifices completely concealed her head as the Hellarms sank beneath the waves carrying its final victim.

Shambling, weakened, Brak turned around. He lurched back to where Mardela lay. Her silver hair was afire in the luminescence of the night. She was breathing lightly, soundly.

Slowly Brak bent down. He picked her up. He turned his scarlet-streaked back on the evil obscenity of Great Tyros.

Brak the barbarian reached the end of the causeway, carrying the rightful queen in his arms. He laid her gently in the punt, cast off, and began to pole back toward the mainland under the light of the stars.

BRAK IN CHAINS

1

The train of seven two-wheeled carts creaked around another corner, and the big, yellow-haired barbarian still standing stubbornly upright in the fourth vehicle let out a growl of surprise.

His scarred hands reached automatically for the cart's side rail, closed. Veins stood out; a long, clotted sword wound down his left forearm began to ooze scarlet again.

One of the small, pelt-clad men crowded into the same cart grumbled when the bigger man accidentally stepped on his foot. In response the barbarian moved his wrists closer together. The hateful chain links hanging between iron wrist cuffs momentarily formed a sort of noose. The barbarian's eyes left no doubt about whose neck the iron noose would fit.

The little, foul-smelling complainer glanced away, looking for sympathy from his companions in the creaking vehicle. The barbarian paid no more attention. Standing tall, he was the only prisoner in all seven carts who did not wear scabrous-looking fur clothing and whose body was not matted with dark, wiry hair.

For a moment the barbarian forgot his seething rage at being captured, subdued, chained, out on the arid plateau two days ago. He was diverted by the sight revealed when the caravan rounded the corner, passing from stifling shadow to the full glare of the sun.

The big man saw a broad avenue, imposingly paved, heat-hazed. The avenue stretched into the distance past shops, public marts, fountained cul-de-sacs where no water ran. At the avenue's far end rose massive buildings of yellow stone, larger and higher than any other structures in the walled city.

The barbarian took note of artfully sculpted idols lining both sides of the avenue at one-square intervals. All the statues were identical; all were of the same transparent crystal. The image was that of a seated human figure with the head of a long-snouted animal. The creature's open jaws held a thin disc. From the ferocity of the expression it was clear that the half beast was about to crunch the disc between its fangs. The image was repeated endlessly, pedestal after crystal-topped pedestal, up the sweltering avenue beneath the cloudless noon sky.

Soldiers of the lord to whose slaving party Brak the barbarian had fallen prey jogged their mounts along the line of seven carts, occasionally cracking short whips. But listlessly. Their dust-covered faces and dust-dulled armor were evidence of the long trek in across the wasteland with the prisoners. On the left wrist of each soldier, from the mounted leader and his subcommanders to the two dozen accompanying footmen, a simple bronze bracelet shot off red-gold glints.

Men and women of the city watched the little caravan from positions beneath awnings and on balconies. Some of the watchers wore elegant robes, others more common cloth.

A boy with one leg missing hobbled forward on a crutch and lobbed a stone at the cart in which Brak rode. The big barbarian stiffened, then realized the stone was not for him, but for the pack of bent, sullen-eyed little men crouched at his calves like stunted trees surrounding one that had grown straight.

The rock struck a man near Brak. He yelped,

jumped up, began to clash his chains and screech at the watchers. His guttural speech was incomprehensible, but not his fury.

Instantly three mounted officers converged on the cart, began to arc their whips onto the backs of the prisoners. The little men cringed and shrieked. The tip of one lash flicked Brak's face. With a deep-chested yell he caught the whip's end and yanked, all his humiliation and self-disgust surfacing as he hauled the surprised officer out of his saddle.

The officer swore, scrabbling in the street on hands and knees. He struggled to free his short-sword. But his fellow officers repaid the barbarian's outburst for him. They pressed their mounts in closer to the cart, whose driver had brought it to an abrupt halt and leaped down out of range of Brak's flailing chains. In a moment the stifling air resounded with the methodical cracking of whips.

Brak made abortive grabs at one or two. Futile. He closed his eyes and gripped the cart rail, trying not to shudder at each new welt laid atop the others crisscrossing his back. He would show them he was not like these dog-men whimpering at his feet. Above all, he would not cry out.

And somehow he would escape the accursed chains dangling between his wrists like the weight of the world—

"Enough."

The voice Brak had heard before sliced through the cracking of the whips, and another sound—the murmurings of the city people as they surged forward to stare at the strange, savage figure of the hulk-shouldered man who wore a lion hide around his middle and his hair in a long yellow braid down his back.

Brak took another lash as the commander shouted again, "*Enough!*"

The whips laid off. Brak opened his eyes to stare into the thin, leather-cheeked face of the young and dusty veteran to whom he had been presented—beaten to his knees—after his capture.

The commander sidled his mount nearer, shook his head wearily:

"You will cast your life away, then? I told you there was a chance for you, outlander—"

"A chance to wear your chains," Brak said and spat.

The spittle struck the commander's breastplate, barely dampening the yellow dust. The commander straightened in his saddle, fingers closing tighter around the butt of his whip.

Then, as if from weariness, or fear, or both, he slumped, letting the insult pass.

"You have the strength to keep fighting back, but I haven't the strength to keep fighting you," the commander sighed. "We'll let someone else drub you into line. Just be thankful you're not like the rest of the filth we caught. Then you wouldn't even have the opportunity of manful service. You'd be put three floors underground, turning the grind wheels for the rest of your life."

"I have no part of this fight between you and your lice-ridden enemies!" Brak snarled, gesturing at the glare-eyed little men crouched around him. His chains clinked. "I was a traveler harming no one. I was set upon—!"

The commander shrugged. "We've gone over it before. I'll not debate. While the foes of Lord Magnus yap around his heels—" Cruelly he kicked one of the little men through the uprights of the cart side. "—our fighting companies need every recruit." He held up his left arm. The bronze bracelet flashed. "I've explained your choice. Wear one of these—or a gravecloth."

He cracked his whip, shouting to the head of the caravan: "Move on, damn you! We've had fourteen days of this sun!"

"And so have we, and more!" a woman cried from the crowd. "If the Children of the Smoke can't bring the Worldbreaker down with spears, they'll bring him down with magic."

The commander glanced down at the crone. "No rain, then?"

"Does it look like we've been cleansed with rain? Refreshed?" someone else yelled. "The Children of the Smoke have bewitched the sky!"

"*Ah!*" The commander gestured angrily. "They have no wizards—"

"Then why does the plain of Magnus burn?" another voice jeered. "Why do the reservoirs go dry? Tell us that, captain!"

Others joined the clamor. Brak thought a riot might erupt on the spot. Nearly a hundred people started shoving and jostling the cart. But the soldiers drove them back with cuts of their whips and jabs of their short-swords.

Wearily Brak reflected that it all had the quality of a nightmare. The heat haze blurred everything, including the snowy ramparts of the Mountains of Smoke far eastward. Those mountains supposedly guarded the approaches of the world's rim and hid the homes of whatever gods ruled these so-called civilized lands.

During the sweltering ride across the plateau to the city Brak had seen once-fertile fields that were parched, their crops stunted. He had listened to grumbling conversations of the soldiers in the heat of evening and learned that his fellow prisoners, all sharp teeth and matted hair and hateful eyes, belonged to a large nomadic tribe from the foothills of those distant mountains. Every few years the tribe tried to gain more lands belonging to the lord who ruled the plateau. It had been Brak's misfortune to be captured and cast among the enemy while he was continuing his long journey southward to golden Khurdisan, where he was bound to seek his fortune—

Some inquisitive soul in the crowd pointed at Brak. "Who is he? Where's he from?"

"He says the wild steppes of the north," a soldier answered.

"Kill him—his presence is another bad omen!" the cry rang back.

"No worse than no rain for a three-month," snarled the soldier, riding on.

The cart driver resumed his place, and the caravan again moved down the dusty avenue between the crystal images of the man-beast with the disc in its mouth. Brak mastered his fury as best he could, though the new and old whip wounds, a webwork on his muscled back, made it difficult. So did the scowls of the soldiers, the taunts of the crowd—

The soldiers had slain his pony in the capture. Broken his broadsword. And chained him. Again he looked yearningly east, toward the cool blue spires rising above the rooftops and the city wall. The Mountains of Smoke, white-crowned. Beyond that barrier, he'd been told, lay down-sloping passes that led into the south—

But he would never see them unless he escaped his chains. Kept his temper—and his life.

He clenched his upper teeth on his lower lip, tasting his own briny sweat, and squinted into the hellish glare of noonday, and saw certain curious things he had not seen before.

2

Most of the citizens abroad in this obviously prosperous city looked wan; frightened. Brak noted another curiosity as the cart rolled past one of the crystal statues. The disc in the mouth of the beast-headed figure had a horizontal crack across its center. He thought this a flaw until he perceived that the discs of several more statues were similarly designed.

He signaled a soldier. The man rode in, but not too close.

Brak asked: "Why is the round thing in the statue's mouth shown broken?"

"Because that is the god-image of Lord Magnus, idiot. Once he held all of creation in his possession—to break or preserve as he saw fit. Now he's an old man. And his wizard, Ool, has no spells against whatever damned magic is being worked on this land."

Brak wiped his sweat-running neck. "You mean no rain."

The soldier nodded. "Without it the reservoirs go empty. The crops perish. It's never happened before. Not in a hundred years, or a hundred again. This was a green and pleasant land before the parching of the skies."

Brak jerked a hand to indicate the bent, hairy heads around his knees. "And the sorcerers of your enemies worked the enchantment?"

"They have no sorcerers!" the soldier rasped back. "Nothing but old medicine women who birth babies."

Or they had no sorcerers until now, Brak thought.

But he kept the retort to himself—because the more closely he looked, the more clearly he could discern the tiredness and terror lurking in the eyes of military man and civilian alike.

Once more he stared down at his chained wrists while the carts lurched nearer the jumble of yellow buildings at the avenue's end. He understood one more thing now. In addition to a tribe of enemies and a magical blight that was decimating city and countryside, the kingdom was also burdened with a lord who thought mightily of himself. Enough, anyway, to build endless replicas of a savage image of himself, and plant in its jaws a representation of the World—

That was what it looked like, eh? Brak had never seen it depicted before.

All the emerging circumstances only heightened his determination to escape. But he would take his time; be cunning and careful—

If he survived this particular ride. He didn't care for the expressions of the men and women lining the avenue. They continued to murmur and point at him. He was an omen; and not a favorable one—

Under those hostile glares a total weariness descended on him suddenly. Maybe this *was* the end after all. Maybe he was fated to die chained and helpless in a country whose strutting lord appeared close to defeat. Worldbreaker indeed! In all the lands he'd traversed thus far, Brak had never heard the name.

Another jarring memory reinforced his new pessimism. What about the toll he had exacted for his capture? How would they settle with him for that?

Head lowered, he was staring at the dusty paving stones rolling by when the shadow of the horse of an attending soldier suddenly vanished.

Shrieks, oaths from both sides of the avenue—

Sudden chittering barks of pleasure from the little prisoners in the carts—

And Brak jerked his head up to gasp while horror shivered his sweaty spine.

In the center of the sky the sun was disappearing.

A smear of gray widened, dulling the light. Tendrils of the strange cloud reached toward all points on the horizon at once—and what had been noon became stifling twilight almost instantly.

The cart horses reacted to the uproar; neighed; pawed the air. One driver jumped down and fled into an alley, not looking back—

There was no wind, no roar of storm. Only that awesome gray cloud spreading and spreading from the apex of heaven. The commotion along the boulevard turned to hysterical tumult.

Darkening, the cloud seemed to race past the city's walls toward the mountains and the wasted plain in the other direction. A young woman fell to her knees, rent the garments over her breasts, shrieked—

Brak whirled. On his left he saw a chilling sight: the gigantic statue of the lord with creation in his mouth began to fill with some dark red substance, translucent; *like blood*—

And the redness was rising in every statue along the avenue.

Kicking his horse, the harried young commander raced up and down the line, lashing his whip to keep the crowd back:

"There's no danger. No danger! It's only another of the enemy's magical apparitions—"

But the crystal images kept darkening, like the sky. The red climbed from the waist toward the head. Noon turned to night. All around Brak the Children of the Smoke still barked and chittered—though many of them now looked fully as frightened as the citizens of the city.

The whipping and the oaths of the soldiers proved futile. The maddened crowds began to surge forward again. Suddenly Brak realized their objective. Another accusing hand pointed his way:

"You brought a polluted pagan through the gates. *That's the reason for all this—!*"

"Stand back, he's a military prisoner!" the commander yelled, just before being buffed from his horse. The mob surged around the cart, all hateful eyes, clawing hands. Brak felt the left wheel lift.

The Children of the Smoke began to gibber and slaver as the cart tilted. Brak knew what would happen. Tumbled into that mob, he'd be torn apart—

As the cart tilted even more sharply, he jumped wide, heedless of where he landed. Both feet came down on a fat man's shoulder. As Brak continued his fall, hands tore at him. But his weight crashed him through to the pavement.

For a moment he was ringed by dirty feet, the hems of dusty robes. Then he glanced up from hands and knees and saw a ring of almost insane faces. Old, young, male, female—and above them a sky turned nearly to ebony—

Peripherally he saw one of the crystal statues. By now it was red to the tips of the beast-head's ears.

"Sacrifice the pagan to drive out the darkness!" a man screamed, lunging.

Brak had no weapon save the length of chain hanging between his hands. He fought to his feet, pressed his wrists together, began to swing them in a circle, whipping them around, faster and faster. The chain opened a man's cheek. Blood gushed. A knife raked

Brak's shoulder. He darted away, keeping the chain swinging.

Another man ventured too close. The end of the chain pulped one eyeball. The man dropped, howling—

And then, it seemed, the splendid boulevard of Lord Magnus the Worldbreaker became utter bedlam.

The mob poured at Brak from all directions, a blur of distorted faces, yapping mouths, glazed eyes that promised murder. So this was to be the end, was it? Dying a victim of some accursed magic in which he had no hand, but for which he was being blamed and punished—

The crystal statues had filled completely, scarlet from pedestal to snout tip. Even the cracked discs of creation were suffused with the evil-looking red. The arch of heaven was dark gray from end to end. Brak abandoned all his former resolve to preserve his life so that he might escape. Now he only wanted to sell his life expensively. If these deranged fools would kill him, they would not do so easily—

Whir and *crack*, the chain whirled. A forearm snapped; a scalp dripped gore. Brak kicked, snarled, spat, worked the chain until he could barely see, so thick was the sweat clogging on his eyelids. Although the sky had blackened, the air had not cooled. He fought in some dim, steaming inferno—

A hand grabbed his ankle. He stamped down, hard. His attacker shrieked, held up ruined, boneless fingers. Whir and *crack*, the chain sliced the air—and suddenly his tormentors began to retreat from his savage figure: from the whip of his long yellow braid; from the flying fur puff at the end of the lion's tail at his waist; from that brain-spattered chain swinging, *scything*—

A way opened. He lunged through full speed, crashing into one of the statue pedestals. Behind him the crowd bayed its anger. The crowd was growing larger as more and more citizens poured in from intersecting avenues. In a moment, backed against the pedestal, Brak was surrounded.

He whirled, leaped high, started to clamber upward, his thighs bloody from the nail marks of hands that clawed him. He gained the top of the pedestal, teetered there, feeling the cool of the crystal against his back. To gain momentum for flailing the chain down at the enraged faces and the hands straining to reach him, he whipped the iron links back over his left shoulder—

The chain smashed against the statue. A prolonged glassy crackling modulated into a sudden loud thunderclap. Light smote Brak's eyes, blinding.

Noon light—

The illusion-cloud in the heavens was gone. Below him, terrorized people dropped to their knees, shielded their eyes—

The chain clinked down across Brak's shoulder. Panting, he curled his toes around the pedestal's edge and squinted across the avenue. There another statue of Lord Magnus the Worldbreaker was crystal-bright, empty of scarlet.

So was every similar image along the avenue.

"You cursed fools—!" Flaying about with his whip, the commander, on horseback again, rode through the mob. "We tried to tell you it was only a wizard's illusion!"

"From where?" someone screamed.

"From the enemy who will conquer!" another cried.

"And *he* dispelled it," the commander said, reining up just below an exhausted Brak leaning against the

image. The commander had a puzzled, almost sad expression on his face. "The chain's blow did it—"

The officer gestured with his whip. Brak craned his buzzing head around, saw a crystalline webbing of cracks running through the bent left knee of the seated figure. Again he felt the clutch of inexplicable dread. The darkness and the rising red had indeed been potent mind-spells. No scarlet ran out from the statue. It was solid.

The commander's smile was feeble. "The end of a short and glorious career," he said. "Now you must be taken to Lord Magnus himself. For the one crime of killing three of my men when you were captured—and the greater crime of profaning an image of the lord."

"*Profaning—!*" Brak screamed, gripping the statue to keep from falling. "The chain broke the statue and the spell and that's an *offense?*"

"Regrettably so. I have no choice but to present you to Lord Magnus for sentence of execution."

In the hot noon silence, while the kneeling, cringing throng peered at Brak through fingers or across the uplifted sleeves of robes, the commander looked sick at heart. For a moment his eyes locked with Brak's, as if begging understanding. Brak was too full of rage. He twisted his head around and spat on the webwork of the smashed crystal. He was done; he knew it. The defilement of the idol brought pleasure.

With another, somehow sad gesture the commander raised his whip to signal his stunned men forming up on the rim of the terrorized mob. He pointed to Brak and said:

"Drag him down."

3

In the largest of the immense buildings he'd glimpsed from afar, Brak the barbarian was conducted into an echoing hall and thrust to his knees by the tense commander. The vast, high-windowed chamber was an inferno of early afternoon shadows. The air was oppressive. Brak had great difficulty breathing.

On the journey to the great complex of yellow stone Brak had several times entertained the idea of trying to break free. But each time he'd decided to wait. Partly out of self-interest; partly from a sort of morbid curiosity. Before his life was taken away, he wanted to set eyes on this lord who styled himself Worldbreaker.

And there was always a faint, formless hope that if he were clever enough—though in what way, he couldn't yet say—he might save himself. The prospect made it seem sensible for him to check his impulse to fight and run.

"You may raise your head to the lord," whispered the decidedly nervous commander who stood next to the kneeling barbarian. Brak obeyed.

All he saw at first was a step. Then another; and eight more, each revealed as his gaze traveled up to a throne that had once been splendid, but was now all green-tinged bronze.

The lower portion of the throne was a massive chair. Its high, solid back rose upward and jutted out over the throne seat to form the gigantic head and snout of the lord's image, complete with cracked disc in its jaws. In the shelter of this canopy sat the Worldbreaker.

A small, thick-chested man. So short his plain, worn soldier's boots barely touched the floor. He wore a military kilt and the familiar bronze bracelet of the army on his left wrist. He looked more like a member of the foot troops than he did a king.

He had a squarish, strong-featured face; much lined. Pure white hair hung to his shoulders. Prepared to be contemptuous, Brak found it hard somehow. The ruler did not adorn himself ostentatiously, though perhaps only because of the heat, which was causing the three or four dozen court officials and military men surrounding the throne's base to shift from foot to foot, mop their sweated cheeks with kerchiefs, and sigh frequently.

Two things about Lord Magnus the Worldbreaker impressed Brak deeply—and alarmed him as well. One was the man's grave, pitiless stare. The other was his body. Calves and thighs, forearms and shoulders and trunk were a war map of the past. Mountain ranges and valleys of scar tissue created a whole geography of battle on the flesh of the ruler. He was, Brak sensed, no commander who had sent his armies ahead to fight. He had led them.

"You may address the lord," said a man who glided into sight from the gloom at one side of the great throne.

"Thanks be to you, oh sexless one," returned the commander, genuflecting. Brak peered at this new personage who had taken a place at the lord's right hand.

The newcomer was a tall, heavily robed man of middle years. He looked overweight. He had an oval, curiously hairless head; opaque eyes; flesh as white as the belly of a new-caught fish. Under the man's basilisk stare Brak shivered.

The commander spoke to the ruler on the throne: "With great Ool's leave given, Lord Magnus, I beg to report a most unfortunate occurrence on the avenue—"

Ool, Brak thought. *So this gelded creature is the ruler's wizard?* An odd specimen indeed. While the others in the chamber were obviously suffering from the heat, Ool's pasty white jowls and ivory forehead remained dry. His hands were completely hidden within the voluminous linen of his crossed sleeves.

Lord Magnus gave a tired nod:

"I saw, Captain Xeraph. From the watch roof I saw the dark heavens and the red-running idols. A footman brought word of the desecration of one of them." The little man's gaze hardened, raking Brak up and down. "This is the pagan slave who worked the damage?"

Suddenly Brak was on his feet. "No, lord. I'm no man's slave. I was set on by your human carrion, caught and trussed up with these—" He rattled his iron chain links.

Ool whispered, "Be silent, barbarian, or you will be slain where you stand."

"I'll be damned before I'll be silent!" Brak yelled.

The hairless wizard inclined his pale head. Three spearmen started clattering down the throne steps, weapons pointed at Brak's chest. The barbarian braced for the attack.

"Hold."

The single, powerful syllable from Lord Magnus checked the spearmen's descent. They swung, looked upward for further instructions. Ool nodded acquiescence, but unhappily; he nibbled at his underlip and treated Brak to a baleful glare.

"You have a ready tongue for a captive," said Lord Magnus in a toneless voice that might have been threatening, or might not. Brak could not tell; nor read that old, scarred countenance. "And you have no knowledge, evidently, that my image is sacred?"

"But shattering it shattered the spell," Brak retorted, glancing pointedly at the pasty-jowled Ool. The man remained impassive. Brak finished, "No one else seemed able to do that."

"Aye, the darkness rolled back," Magnus agreed. "The darkness which cannot be–" His mouth wrenched, a quick, sour imitation of a smile. "–since our mortal enemies have no enchanters to work such spells. None at all! Therefore we cannot be plagued. What happened is impossible–*everything* is impossible!" he shouted, slamming a horn-hard palm on the throne's curved arm.

At that moment Brak sensed just how much rage must be seething under that gnarled old exterior. It was a rage like his own. Although Brak did not care for this lord and never would, he did not precisely hate him, either. It was a puzzling circumstance he did not fully understand.

Lord Magnus went on, "The Children cannot work wizardries against us, therefore all I see is a deception. The water channels dry and silted–a deception. The people maddened and near to revolt–deception. The noon heavens like midnight–and a chain that breaks the illusion–no, none of it's real. Perhaps not even you, eh, outlander?"

Brak rattled his chains. "Take these off and I'll show you my hands are real. You'll see how real when they close on the throats of your jackals."

The commander, Captain Xeraph, gulped audibly. Gasps and oaths rippled through the crowd clustered near the throne. Swords snicked out of scabbards. Abruptly Lord Magnus laughed.

The sound was quick, harsh—and stunned everyone, including the big barbarian. With effort, he stared the ruler down. Neither man blinked.

"You seem determined to die quickly," Lord Magnus said.

"It appears I have no choice in the matter, lord." Mocking: "I violated your holy image—"

"And," put in the hairless Ool, his calm tone belying the animosity Brak saw in his eyes, "if our intelligence may be trusted, slew three of Captain Xeraph's best when they took you prisoner."

"Aye," Brak nodded. "Because they had no reason to seize me."

"The fact that you crossed my boundary marker is reason enough," Lord Magnus advised.

"To you, lord. To a traveler bound to Khurdisan—no."

Magnus lifted one scar-crusted hand, scratched his sweaty chin where a beard stubble already showed white after the day's razoring. "Cease your glowering and grimacing, kindly! Don't you wonder why you're not dead by now? You apparently fail to recognize a chance to survive when it's presented to you."

In the little man's dark eyes Brak saw nothing he could comprehend. A plot was weaving. But what kind of plot he could not tell.

Still something in him seized at the half-offered promise. He felt hope for the first time.

The ghoul-white face of Ool the sexless looked stark. *Careful,* Brak thought. *Do not appear over-eager—*

He licked his sweaty lips, said:

"I do not understand the lord's meaning, that's true. But I understand little or nothing of what has befallen me. I tell you again—there was no reason for me to be imprisoned. Or brought to your city in bondage."

"You deny that a man can be slain for killing three soldiers of a land through which he travels?" Magnus asked.

"I was attacked!"

"You deny a man can be punished for desecrating the sacred law of such a land?"

"I never broke your image on purpose. Only accidentally, while trying to save myself from the mob."

"And you broke the darkness too," Magnus mused. Suddenly a finger stabbed out, pointing down. Brak saw that the finger was a toughened stub at the end; lopped off at the first knuckle long ago.

"What is your name, outlander? Where did you journey from? Most important—how did you come by the power that broke the darkness?"

The big barbarian answered, "Lord, I'm called Brak. My home was once the northern steppes. My people cast me out for mocking their gods—"

"Ah, you make a habit of that!" said Magnus, the corners of his mouth twisting again.

"When the rules of such gods defy a man's own good sense, yes. I am bound south for Khurdisan—or I was," he added with a smoldering glance at the uncomfortable Captain Xeraph. "As to why and how I was able to rend the darkness in the sky—" *Careful!* He spaced the next words with deliberate slowness. "—I ask leave not to say."

Ool chuckled, a dry, reedy sound. "In other words, you confirm that you have no real powers."

Staring fiercely at the wizard, Brak replied, "I neither confirm it nor deny it, magician. After I am dead, you may make up your own mind."

Again Magnus laughed. He studied Brak closely, said at last:

"But perhaps—as I hinted—there is another way. For the first time I am besieged by forces against which my host and my chariots will not avail. You are a bold man, Brak barbarian. Strong-looking to boot. You *seem* to have thaumaturgic skills—whether by training or by accident, you don't care to reveal. Very well—"

Magnus stood. Brak realized just how short the old man really was. But his ridged shoulders and scar-marked belly looked tough as iron.

"You cannot guess the extremes to which we have gone to overcome this plague of dryness. A plague that can destroy this kingdom as the pitiful clubs and daggers of the Children of the Smoke never could before. So despite your crimes, my rude friend—and because you staved off carnage in the streets—I will strike you a bargain."

Cold and shrewd, the eyes of the Worldbreaker pierced down from the sweaty gloom around the throne.

"You will not die. You will not wear chains—"

Brak's heart almost burst at the sudden, unexpected reprieve; then he heard the jarring conclusion:

"If you can bring down the rain."

"Bring down the—?"

He wanted to laugh. He couldn't. He was too appalled by the sudden snapping of the trap.

"Open the heavens!" Magnus exclaimed, his voice genuinely powerful now. "Darken the skies—but this time, so they flood the land with downpour. Unbind the spell of the Children of the Smoke—whatever it is, and from wherever it comes—and you'll neither die nor wear chains again. That is my concession and my promise, Brak barbarian. Whether you have true or only chance powers, we shall now discover. I warn you, none has succeeded so far in undoing the plague spell. My own wizard is helpless—" A lifted hand made Ool bristle; more softly, Magnus went on. "—though not through any lack of daily effort and industry, I must hasten to add. Now—"

He directed his gaze at the astounded young commander.

"While we test the barbarian, Captain Xeraph, you shall be his guardian and constant companion. Let him not out of your sight for a moment, or your own life is forfeit."

The commander went white. Brak started to protest that he had been lured into a hopeless snare, but Magnus gestured:

"I have already given you a great concession. Keep silent and ask for nothing more."

He turned his back, starting to leave by circling the throne. After a quick glance down the stairs at Brak, the eunuch Ool plucked his lord's forearm. Annoyed, Magnus stopped.

Ool leaned in, whispered. Magnus pondered. Then he wheeled around, said to Brak:

"One further condition—and a wise one, I think. You have two days and two nights to make it rain, no more."

Again Brak sensed the old fighter's desperation; glimpsed it in his eyes just before the Worldbreaker vanished behind the throne, Ool gliding after him, a white specter—

Leaving Brak to reflect dismally that he would have been better off to have been killed outright.

4

"Balls of the gods, will you pick a piece and move it?" shouted Captain Xeraph, jumping up. He stalked through the arch to the little balcony overlooking the city and, a floor below, a courtyard shared by four barracks buildings.

Perched on a stool much too small for his bulk, Brak looked with bleary eyes at the out-of-humor officer pacing back and forth just beyond the arch. Xeraph was stripped down to his kilt. Both occupants of the tiny officer's apartment in the yellow stone complex were sticky with perspiration, even though the sun had simmered out of sight hours ago. But another light limned the officer's profile as he leaned on the balcony rail and gazed at the night city.

The rooftops were outlined by red glares from half a dozen locations. The roaring of mobs and the crashes of mass destruction carried through the still air. Xeraph's right hand strayed absently to the bracelet on his left wrist as he stared at the fires with something akin to longing.

The captain's apartment consisted of two narrow rooms. Both rooms were sparsely furnished. But the addition of a pallet for Xeraph's semiprisoner badly cramped the main room. The master of the quarters swung suddenly, glaring—another challenge for Brak to get on with his move.

The huge, yellow-haired man picked up the tail of his lion clout, used it to wipe sweat from his nose, then draped it over one muscled thigh so it hung between his legs. He reached down for the wine jar beside his bare feet.

He tilted the jug, drank deeply of the dry red wine, heedless of the way it dripped down his chin onto his massive chest. Putting the jar aside again, he peered fuzzily at the playing board set on a low block of stone.

The board featured a pattern of squares in two colors. On the squares sat oddly carved wood pieces of different designs. Half the pieces were lacquered dark green. The others had been left unfinished.

For two hours Captain Xeraph had been trying to teach him the confusing game. Eating little and drinking much after the disastrous interview with Magnus earlier in the day, Brak had no head for it. Even sober, he had decided, he probably couldn't comprehend it.

But Xeraph was so obviously upset by his enforced confinement with a prisoner that Brak made one more effort. He picked up one of his pieces, the one named—let's see, could he remember?—the fortress.

Xeraph watched him slide the piece to the adjoining square. With a curse the captain stormed back into the room, snatched up the piece, and shook it in Brak's face:

"This is the wizard, you idiot! The wizard cannot move in that pattern. I must have explained it ten times!"

Brak's temper let go. Growling, he lifted a corner of the playing board. Several pieces fell off. With a sweep of his thick arm he scattered the rest, then flung the board on the floor.

"Take your playthings and throw 'em in the pit!" Brak shouted, his eyes ugly. The hateful chains clinked between his wrists.

For a moment he thought Captain Xeraph would

grab his short-sword from the scabbard hanging on a wall peg. Xeraph's neck muscles bunched. But he managed control. He sighed a long, disgusted sigh:

"I shouldn't expect some unlettered foreigner to master a game played by civilized gentlemen. But gods! I'm already sick of tending you—!"

"I didn't ask to be penned up here!" Brak screamed back, and again it seemed as if the two would go for each other's throat. Then, sighing again, Xeraph slumped, as if the heat, the effort of argumentation, were too much.

He sprawled on Brak's pallet while the latter stood glowering and fingering the chain.

"Well, one night's almost done," Xeraph said in a gloomy tone. "One more, and two days, and Magnus will take your head." His eyes sought Brak's. He almost sounded sorrowful: "You have no spells to bring rain, do you?"

Brak's answer was a terse, "Of course not. Why the darkness lifted when I smashed the idol, I don't know. Your lord's a desperate man—he admitted it himself. I have seen men in similiar predicaments grow rash and foolish. That's what happened when your lord offered me that ridiculous bargain for my life."

Xeraph clucked his tongue. "The lord's too old—that's what they're all saying. Believe me, Magnus has no lack of courage—"

"His scars prove that."

"—but for once, the odds are too overwhelming. He can't cope with the magic with which the Children have cursed us."

"Nor, apparently, can his own wizard, despite those efforts to which Magnus referred. How does the eunuch try to bring down rain and end the drought?"

The officer shrugged. "To watch Ool do whatever he does—mix potions, wail at the sky—is forbidden to all but a few young boys who attend him. They are specially selected and, I might add, perverted." Xeraph's mouth quirked in distaste. "Every day Ool rides out in his chariot, that much I know. He goes toward the channel that once brought sweet rainwater from the lower slopes of the Mountain of Smoke." Xeraph gestured eastward. "Somewhere out there, Ool tried to undo the curse—in secret." The captain concluded sarcastically, "Like to discover some of his methods, would you?"

"They sound worthless. On the other hand, since I have no powers of my own, I've thought of the idea. I don't intend to spend the rest of the allotted time pacing this room and drinking myself into oblivion."

That amused Xeraph. "Oh, you think you can improve upon Ool's performance, do you? Acquire magical skills like that?" He snapped his fingers.

Brak scowled. "I doubt it. But there must be an answer somewhere. And if it lies in magic, what better place to begin the search than with Ool?"

"You don't give up easily," Xeraph said, not without admiration. Brak simply stared at the litter of game pieces scattered around his thoroughly dirty feet. Xeraph harrumphed. "Brak, there is no answer! Except this. The rain won't come. And you'll die. Then the rest of us. This time—" Restless, he rose and wandered back to the balcony. "—this time I think the Worldbreaker himself will be broken. And all of his kingdom in the bargain."

Suddenly Xeraph's voice grew louder: "They're already going mad! Drinking, rioting, setting fires—"

"And you feel you should be out there helping to quell it."

Xeraph spun. "Yes! That duty, I understand.

This—" His gesture swept the lamplit chamber resentfully. "It's fool's work."

Speaking out of genuine feeling, Brak said, "Captain, I am sorry the lot fell to you."

"No apologies," Xeraph cut him off. "I obey orders. It's a bad twist of fate's twine, that's all. We've had nothing else for months—why should I expect a change?"

Once more the young officer leaned on the railing, staring in dismay at the sullen scarlet silhouettes of the city's rooftops. His eyes picked up red reflections; simmered with frustration. Hopelessness.

Brak resumed his place on the stool. He picked up a wooden piece which, if his wine-buzzing head served him, represented a male ruler. He asked:

"Has Lord Magnus no trusted advisers to help point the way out of this difficult situation? No generals—?"

"He is the general," Xeraph returned. "He is the government, the chief judge—everything. Before, his shoulders have always been strong enough, his mind quick enough—"

The statement somehow fitted with Brak's appraisal of the tough little warrior. The barbarian studied the piece in his sweat-glistening palm a moment longer.

"The lord hasn't even a wife to counsel him?" he wanted to know.

"He did, many years ago—why go into all this?" Xeraph said irritably.

"I don't know," Brak admitted. "Except that I don't want to be killed."

Xeraph managed an exhausted smile. "That, at least, is something we have in common."

"We were talking of Magnus. He has no sons—?"

Xeraph shook his head. "No issue at all." Briefly,

then, he narrated the story of Magnus' consort, a queen whose name he could not even recall because she had died forty years earlier, well before Xeraph himself had been born. But legend said the lord's wife had been exceedingly lovely and desirable.

Lord Magnus had been away on a campaign to harry the Children of the Smoke, who were making one of their abortive advances into his territory. A soldier in the small detachment left behind to garrison the city—"name unknown, identity unknown," Xeraph commented—entered the apartment of the lord's wife by stealth one night. Presumably drunk, he raped her.

"The lady cried out, and the terrified fool cut her throat. There was a great melee in the darkness. The soldier was pursued. Another captain who died only a six-month ago was on duty in the palace at the time and swore he caught the offender for a moment. Claimed he ran him through with a spear. But the man ultimately escaped in the confusion—to perish of his wound in some back alley, presumably. His corpse was never found. And as I say, his name remains unknown to this day. Magnus was so overcome with grief, he could never take another woman to his side, except for serving girls for single nights of pleasure. Even that stopped five or six years ago," Xeraph finished unhappily.

Brak set the lord piece aside in favor of the piece he had moved wrongly before: the wizard.

"And this court magician—do you think he serves the Worldbreaker well?"

Xeraph shrugged. "If not well, then faithfully and diligently, at least. You heard the lord say as much. Ool was a wandering shaman, I'm told. He came to court a long time ago, and stayed. Until now he's always seemed proficient in minor spells and holy rituals. But this particular curse has proved too large for his powers—as it has for the lord's. And so we'll be destroyed—"

"Unless it rains."

Captain Xeraph glanced away.

Brak walked to the balcony, looking out into the flame-shot dark. Thinking aloud, he said, "Perhaps I would indeed do well to observe this Ool at work. It's possible I might find inspiration! Discover powers I never knew I had—"

At first Xeraph's expression showed surprise. This was quickly replaced by new annoyance:

"I told you, Brak—observance of the wizard's private mysteries is forbidden. Just as entering his quarters is forbidden."

Brak shook his head. The long yellow braid bobbed gently against his lash-marked back. "When my life is forfeit, nothing's forbidden."

Again Xeraph couldn't contain a half-admiring smile: "Gods, what a determined lout you are. In better times Lord Magnus could use a hundred like you in his fighting companies."

"I mean to be free of these chains, captain, not serve your lord or any other."

"What about the lord who takes life?" Xeraph retorted. "It's him you'll be serving at sunset the day after tomorrow! Look—why risk more trouble with Ool? You've admitted you have no arcane talents—"

"But I repeat, I won't sit and wait to be executed. If you can think of a better idea than observing the wizard, tell me and I'll do it."

"We'll do it," Xeraph corrected. "Remember, if I lose sight of you—" Matter-of-factly he stroked an index finger across his sweat-blackened throat. In the distance another huge crash rent the night. A column of flame and sparks shot heavenward. Somewhere a mob bayed like a beast.

Finally Brak gave a crisp nod. "Well, then—tomorrow, when I'm rested—and sober—I mean to find this water channel where master Ool tries his futile spells. You can either let me blunder there alone, or you can go with me and fulfill the lord's charge that you keep watch on me."

"You could never pass the city gates without me."

"Don't be too sure, captain."

Slowly Xeraph wiped his palms down his lean thighs. He gave Brak a steady look. Not defying him. Testing:

"But what if I say no to your excursion, my friend?"

"I will go anyway."

"I might stop you."

"You might try," Brak replied softly.

In truth he felt that the plan was exactly like all other plans afloat in the capital of Magnus the World-breaker: worthless. But he had no other alternative in mind.

He felt like an animal hunted by mounted men and dogs. With certain doom at his heels he was still unwilling to stop and await death. He preferred motion—even though it was empty of solid hope or solid purpose. At least doing something might temporarily dispel the morbid thoughts of his future—

Besides, perhaps the scheme wasn't so foolish after all. The wizard Ool presented curious contradictions. If he had entrenched himself at the court with his magical proficiency in the past, why had his talents suddenly proved wanting? Having experienced first-hand the abilities of both lesser and greater wizards, Brak could understand how Ool might not be competent to overcome the drought spell. Yet it was still odd that none around Lord Magnus raised the question of why Ool failed. They merely accepted it.

Perhaps they were too occupied with the tangible, pressing dangers of an advancing enemy and a populace in near-revolt. Perhaps the outside viewpoint of a stranger was required to see past distractions to simple, essential questions—

Such as the puzzle of Ool. Brak's hard, sweating face confirmed his resolve concerning the matter.

All at once Captain Xeraph bowed to that; and laughed:

"Damn you for an insolent rogue, Brak—all right, we'll go. At sunrise." He kicked at the fallen playpiece and added, with a smile that bore no malice, "It can't be any more useless than trying to teach a thick-skulled foreigner this noble game."

Brak smiled a bleak smile in return and reached for the wine jar. Out in the city more burning buildings began to fall, crashing—

5

The sun ate cruelly at Brak's body, promising painful burns by nightfall. With Captain Xeraph he was crouched at the foot of a ridge some distance east of the city. The wall, some rooftops, and columns of smoke could still be seen through clouds of dust blowing across empty, desiccated fields.

Like Brak, Captain Xeraph had cast aside the coarse cowled cloak each had worn to slip through the city gates shortly after dawn. Xeraph's presence had permitted them to leave with only a brief questioning. The discarded cloaks lay under a stone now, snapping and fluttering at their feet.

Xeraph wore a plain artisan's kilt. Except for his short-sword and the bronze bracelet which could not be removed, there was nothing to mark him as a military man.

He looked fearful as Brak peered toward the jumbled boulders along the ridgetop. Both men could clearly hear the strange sounds coming from the far side.

Brak knew why Xeraph was upset. What they were about to do was forbidden. Yet as Brak listened, the sounds seemed more odd than alarming; a mystery more than a menace.

He heard the creak of wheels; the rattle of hoofs. Now louder, then fading—exactly like the furious thudding of beaten drumheads. A voice chanted an incomprehensible singsong.

"I am going up to look, captain," Brak said.

Xeraph swallowed. "Very well, we'll—" Abruptly: "No, I'll stay here."

He shoved the point of his sword against Brak's throat. The barbarian edged away quickly but carefully. Xeraph's trembling hand might cause an accident.

"Don't get out of sight, understand?"

Then Xeraph darted a nervous glance around the sere horizon. Further east stood a farmstead, abandoned in the blowing dust. Hoofs and wheels, drums and chanting grew louder again. Brak gave a tight nod, turned, and began to clamber up the hillside.

He moved cautiously, with the craft of the steppe-born hunter. Twice he stopped still and cursed, as the damnable chains between his wrists clinked too loudly.

He turned once to see Captain Xeraph staring up at him with an absolutely terrified expression. Brak hardened his heart and continued his climb. Whatever lay on the other side of the ridge was not sacred to him. And in his travels toward Khurdisan's golden crescent in the far south he had encountered many marvels and enchantments. He did not precisely fear the sight of an inept wizard.

At length he worked himself between two boulders, his lips already dry and cracked from the heat. He looked out and down—

And blinked in astonishment.

As Xeraph had said, an immense, stone-lined channel lay below. It stretched east toward the mountains, west toward the city. The channel was filled with blowing dust.

Along a track on the far side an imposing gold-chased chariot drawn by four white horses raced at furious speed. Brak counted five people in the oversized car, in addition to the driver.

Gripping the car's front rail, his voluminous robes flying behind him, stood Ool the magician, head thrown back. It was Ool uttering that weird, ululating chant.

Behind him, swaying and knocking against one another, was a quartet of boys with pudgy pink legs, ringleted hair, soft hands, and generally feminine appearance. One had a pair of drums suspended on a strap around his neck. Another pounded the skin drumheads with padded beaters. A third picked up lengths of wood from the floor of the car and set them afire with a torch. The fourth threw the fresh-lit firebrands out of the car while Ool continued to chant.

Brak swore a foul oath. The whole expedition had been wasted. He had seen a similar ceremony in his youth in the wild lands of the north—and if this was all Ool could muster to open the heavens and relieve the drought, he was a poor wizard indeed.

The chariot continued to race along beside the channel, traveling a short way eastward before wheeling back again. Ool kept up his singsong chant. The drums pounded. The torches arched out of the car every which way—

Despairing, Brak watched only a few moments longer. Just as the chariot completed its course away on his left and turned back toward his vantage point, he prepared to rejoin Xeraph. The chariot swept along beside the channel—and a gust of wind caught the magician's gown; flattened his sleeves back against his forearms. Suddenly Brak's belly flip-flopped. He stared through the sweat running off his eyebrows. Stared and stared as the chariot raced nearer, boiling dust out behind—

Firebrands scattered sparks. The drums *thud-*

thudded. Brak squinted against the sun glare, watching Ool's hands gripping the rail of the car—

As the chariot swept past, a thin suspicion became an alarming possibility.

The chariot thundered on, the drum throbs and hoof rattles and wheel creaks diminishing again. Brak scrambled up, avoiding Captain Xeraph's anxious gaze from the bottom of the ridge.

What should he do? Go instantly to Lord Magnus?

No, he'd never be believed. He was an outlander; with no status except the useless one of prisoner. Automatically he would be counted a liar.

And if Ool heard of an accusation, he would probably move against the barbarian in some secret way. Have him slain before the time limit expired—

Yet Brak knew he had to act. Gazing into the dusty sunlight, he let his mind cast up images of the magician in the chariot. White cheeks. Jowls jiggling, soft and flabby. And the hands; the momentarily bared hands and forearms—those Brak saw most vividly of all.

Not a little frightened, he clambered down. Xeraph clutched his arm:

"What did you see?"

"Trumpery," Brak said with a curt wave, wanting no hint of his suspicion to show on his face. "Magic such as the pathetic shamans of my own land practiced in hopes of changing the weather—"

Briefly he described the sights he'd observed—except for Ool's revealed hands.

Captain Xeraph was baffled by the details Brak reported. He asked for further explanation.

"They beat drums and throw torches helter-skelter to simulate thunder and lightning. Along with that, Ool howls some spell or other. The idea is to summon storms by imitating them. I've never seen it work before, and I venture it won't work now."

Because, whispered a cold little serpent voice in his mind, *it is not meant to work.*

"Captain Xeraph," he said, "we must immediately—"

He stopped. Would this plain soldier who dealt in simple, fundamental concepts such as marching formations and use of weapons understand what he did not fully understand himself? Certainly he could not prove so much as one jot of his suspicion—yet. An accusation now, even presented to one such as Xeraph who, Brak felt, half trusted him, would only bring ridicule.

Brow furrowed, Xeraph stared at him. "Must what, outlander? Finish what you started to say."

At last Brak knew what he must do. *Tonight.* Tonight would provide the only hours of darkness left.

But as he realized what he had to do—and do alone—he felt dismayed. If he took the risk, followed out the sketchy plan already in mind, he might put Captain Xeraph's life in jeopardy. And while he would never be fond of any captor, Xeraph was at least more agreeable than most.

Still his own life was in jeopardy too. That made the difference.

"We must immediately return to the city," Brak concluded, a hasty lie. He felt the shame of a betrayer; the dread of the night's work waiting. "I saw nothing but a eunuch doing child's magic."

Xeraph looked relieved. They crept away from the ridge. The drumming and chanting and chariot clatter faded.

Cloaked again, they trudged west in the heat. Each was silent, but for different reasons.

6

A night and a day. Like some drunken balladeer's refrain, the words kept coming to Brak's thoughts as he lay tensely on his pallet, counting time. *A night and a day—*

Outside, steamy darkness; his final night was perhaps half gone already. On the morrow he would have no more chance. The light of the simmering sky would make his desperate gamble impossible. *A night and a day to make it rain—*

No. He amended in the grim silence of his thoughts, *a night—this night—to discover why it does* not *rain.*

At last the stertorous breathing of Captain Xeraph subsided in the adjoining room. Brak rolled over, raised himself on an elbow, then bunched his legs beneath him.

Slowly he raised to a standing position. His body was already slicked with perspiration. The fall of the sun had brought no relief, no coolness. Through the arch that led to the apartment's regular bedchamber, the sounds of Xeraph thrashing came again.

As he stole barefoot toward the peg where Xeraph's sword scabbard hung, Brak tried to remember the position of the hilt; about halfway up the wall, wasn't it? He kept moving, cautiously—

Another pace.

Another.

Three more to go.

Then two.

He froze.

Soldiers were crossing the courtyard below the balcony. Three or four of them, he couldn't be certain. They were singing an obscene barracks ditty.

At last a heavy door closed. Brak moved again, wondering that the men of Lord Magnus had the heart to sing while the red of last night's fires still flickered throughout one quarter of the sky. A vast tenement section had been set ablaze, Xeraph had reported after the evening meal. The flaming devastation had yet to be contained—

Well, perhaps the soldiers of Magnus drank heaviest and sang loudest when they were powerless against certain defeat.

He listened. The courtyard was silent.

He lifted his hand, groping for the hilt of the short-sword. But, somehow, while his attention had been distracted by the noises below, he had lost his precise sense of distances in the dark. Reaching out, he felt the back of his right hand collide suddenly with the hilt while his fingers closed on empty air. The scabbard knocked the wall. Loudly—

For a moment he held absolutely still, breath sucked in. But the damage was done. Wakened by the noisy thump against the intervening wall, Xeraph muttered a questioning monosyllable.

Brak didn't debate with himself for long. There would be no arguing with Xeraph. The captain would forbid what he'd planned. He jerked the short-sword from the scabbard, heedless of the racket of his chain. He pivoted and plunged toward the balcony.

Behind him he heard Xeraph thrash, call out. Then Brak caught the *slap-slap* of running feet.

One thick, scarred leg hooked over the low balcony wall as Xeraph rushed from the darkened apartment. Both hands on the hilt Brak whipped up the short-sword, turning the blade just so and hammering it down in what he hoped would be a felling but not wounding blow.

Again he cursed his bad luck. He could tell the blow was misaimed. Xeraph was moving too fast, cursing him as a damned trickster—

The sword-flat thwacked and slid away. Captain Xeraph let out a loud, hurt cry as he crumpled.

Brak listened again, hoping that the doorkeeper on the floor below was drowsing in his booth. But again good luck eluded him. The distant rapping of boots signaled the doorkeeper climbing the inner stairs to investigate the cry.

Brak faced a terrible decision. Remain—and fall. Or go on and leave Xeraph to be discovered. Minus his prisoner. The barbarian knew what Xeraph's punishment would be—

In the hot darkness Brak's face hardened. He would try to complete his night errand swiftly. Come back to Xeraph in time.

But if he failed—

Well, better not to think of that.

Xeraph was a decent, kindly jailer. But something deeper and darker within the huge barbarian swept that consideration aside. Something deeper, darker—and as heavy as the chains between his wrists.

The doorkeeper hammered outside Xeraph's apartment. A querulous voice inquired whether something was amiss. Xeraph, a fallen lump, stirred. Groaned. Brak's face was pitiless, a mask for his regret as he swung his other leg over and dropped toward the courtyard.

He would save Xeraph if he could. But, above all, he would not live in chains.

7

Infuriated by the series of unlucky circumstances that had so far wrecked all but the basic thrust of his plan, Brak landed in a jarring crouch. He did his best to muffle the clinking links against his naked belly, at the same time maneuvering to keep from being cut by the sword.

He heard the doorkeeper knocking more insistently now. He bolted for the far side of the quadrangle and a passage that would lead to a second, larger yard in the palace complex.

The knocking and shouting continued. Brak dodged into the passage just as a lamp was lit in another officer's apartment. The whole area would be awake soon. Damn and damn again!

Racing down the passage, he checked where the wall ended. He flattened his naked back against stone that still radiated heat. Behind him more lamps bobbed. Shouts of genuine alarm were being raised.

He forced his concentration ahead. Saw a tired, limping soldier crossing the dark square on guard duty. The man walked with infernal slowness. Would he hear the commotion—?

Brak's breath hissed in and out of his lungs, a low, bestial sound. His eyes picked up some of the scarlet glare in the cloudless sky. Like a preying animal, he watched and counted time's destructive passage. If the soldier reacted to the distant noise from the officer's quarters—or if he about-faced to recross the square instead of proceeding on rounds elsewhere, Brak intended to kill him.

But the man did vanish inside a lantern-hung doorway. Perhaps he'd heard the racket and didn't care. Perhaps he wanted a drink of cool wine to break the night's sticky monotony. Whatever the reason, he was gone.

Whipping his head left and right, Brak checked for anyone else who might be observing him. He saw no one. He broke from cover, dashed toward the outer staircase of the two-story yellow building directly opposite.

On the second floor of that structure, he had learned via a casual inquiry to Xeraph, Ool the eunuch had his quarters. The floor below was occupied by the two dozen pink-lipped boys who served him. No one else was permitted to enter the building, Xeraph said. No other servants. Not even Lord Magnus.

Panting, Brak reached the exterior steps, crouched at the bottom, peering upward. He expected to see a guard posted on the terrace entrance to Ool's apartment. He saw no one.

Taking a tight grip on the sword's hilt, he began to climb, muffling the clinking chain as best he could. Time was running too fast for complete caution—

He still had no clear notion of what he expected to find, should he be lucky enough to penetrate Ool's private quarters. Evidence of treachery—but in what form? He couldn't predict.

Still he was convinced his suspicions had some foundation. So he took the stairs three at a time.

By the time he neared the top, he wondered whether Ool's position was so secure, and his powers so feared, that he needed no personal guards. Somehow Brak couldn't believe that. Yet, conscious of Xeraph's peril, he didn't pause to ponder the question—

He reached the terrace, immediately turned right toward a doorless arch where thin hangings stirred slowly. Deep in the dark of the apartment beyond he saw white light flicker. He heard a small, hollow rumbling, mysterious and inexplicable, that somehow made his spine crawl.

A slithering noise spun him around.

He sucked in a startled breath at the sight of one—no, two—gods, *three* of the plump-faced boys rising from the shadow of the terrace railing. Had they been squatted there all along? Because of his haste and the darkness Brak had missed them.

Their peculiar bright eyes glistened with red reflections from the sky. One boy giggled, shuffled a sandaled foot forward. Pressed against him, his companions followed suit.

The three advanced another step with those gleeful, half-mad expressions on their faces. *Were they drugged assassins—?*

Wary, awaiting attack, Brak was in one way reassured. Ool's quarters were, in fact guarded. Because he had something to conceal?

In a wet, lisping voice, one of the round-faced trio said, "No one may enter to disturb the slumber of the sexless one."

"I think this says otherwise," Brak growled, giving the short-sword a flourish.

From the apartment he heard that preternatural rumbling again. The white-fleshed boys interlocked their hands and laughed at him. High-pitched, feminine giggles.

They were not armed. *But they were laughing at him!*

He backed up a pace, dread grabbing at his bowels. The trio kept mincing toward him, hands clutching hands. The faces suddenly glowed paste-white, illuminated by that strange radiance flaring inside the apartment—

Somehow Brak's eyes misted. He blinked. No, the trouble was not in his eyes. A fog seemed to be forming around the boys.

The middle boy opened his mouth to laugh again. And Brak's brain shrieked nameless terror as that mouth began to *grow*—

Began to stretch upward, downward, both sides simultaneously, becoming a huge, spectral monstrosity with sharp, filed teeth that gleamed wet with spittle. *Teeth the size of Brak's own head*—

Suddenly there were three giant, slavering mouths, each swollen outward from the head of a boy. There was a mouth on his left, another on his right, one directly ahead—all three arching forward to bite his skull and crack it—

Enchantments! Brak's mind screamed. *Illusions! They need no weapons because Ool taught them to guard with spells*—

Yet his own terror was real. So was the horrendous *craack* as the gigantic, disembodied central mouth clashed its teeth together, almost taking off his left arm.

Brak could see nothing of the trio of boys now. Only the formless mist in which the distended mouths were the sole perverted reality. Huge pink-lipped maws, clicking and grimacing and coming closer, left and right ahead, *closer*—

The left mouth clashed its teeth three times. Then an immense, serpentine tongue shot from the maw and licked the lower lip in anticipation. A spittle gob the size of a fist dripped from the tongue's end—

Mesmerized with dread, Brak barely heard the noise on his right. He jerked his head around just in time to see the mouth arching over him, the gigantic teeth straining apart in preparation for the death bite. Brak's brain howled his mortal fear. Yet something else within him still cried out:

Spells! Mind-dreams! You have seen them before! FIGHT THEM—

Both hands on the blade hilt, he somehow found strength to hurl himself beneath the closing jaw—CRAACK—and stab into the mist as far as his chained arms would permit. Somewhere in that ghostly whorl of mind-smoke the tip of his sword struck solid flesh—

A human shriek, bubbling and wild, roiled the smoke suddenly. The grinding mouth that had almost closed on him vanished.

The images of the other two began to shimmer and grow dim. Through the smoke he perceived a dying boy sprawled on the terrace flags, black-looking blood pouring out of his stabbed throat.

The mouth facing Brak flew at him, sharp-filed teeth wide open. But this time Brak fought his own hysteria more successfully, braced his legs, and stabbed into the mist beneath the apparition—

And it too vanished, simultaneously with a cry of mortal hurt.

One phantom left—and that image was feeble. Through the vile, immense tongue Brak glimpsed the reddened heavens of the city. He tossed his sword to his left hand, extended both arms as far as he could, and killed the unseen boy behind the snapping mouth—

Which shrank and puffed away, leaving three sad, suetlike bodies in a bloodied heap.

Gasping, Brak wiped sweat from his eyes. His heart pounded so heavily that it almost brought physical pain. Surely the cries of the boy-guards with their devilish mind projections had wakened the sleeper in the apartment. And others near the square—

Brak peered over the stone railing, saw the lone soldier pacing listlessly again. The only sounds the big barbarian heard were the drag of the soldier's boots and—behind him—that strange, hollow crashing that reverberated into stillness.

He leaned down, prodded one of the forlorn corpses. His fingers came away sticky with warm blood. No, the obscene mouths had not been real. But the briefly invisible bodies that had tasted his iron had been real. That in itself was a reassurance of sanity, giving him the courage to turn, take three steps, raise his shortsword to touch the edge of one of the hangings, and lift it—

Again that eerie white light flickered and danced deep in the apartment's gloom.

Brak tried to discern the light's source. It seemed to radiate from behind another drapery. But he couldn't be sure.

He listened again.

Silence. Where was Ool?

If Brak had somehow slain the evil boys without a sound, perhaps the wizard had not been awakened. Perhaps all the noises he'd heard during the struggle had been illusions too. The thought emboldened him to the point of taking one step past the hanging. From the concealment of the distant drapery the hollow booming sounded once more.

Brak's backbone crawled as a sibilant voice spoke:

"Even in sleep, my mind is linked with those of my protectors. Their power comes from my thoughts, you see. When they died, I wakened. To give you a fitting reception, my curious outlander."

On the last word spoken by the unseen Ool, the short-sword in Brak's right hand burned. He screamed and let go.

The blade flew toward the ceiling, lighting the whole splendidly furnished apartment for one bizarre instant. The sword turned molten, dripping. Dollops of glowing fire struck the apartment's tiles and burned smoking pits into them.

Brak dodged back from the fire-shower, seeing beyond it the hairless body of Ool standing beside his canopied bed, naked save for a loin-wrapping of linen that matched the whiteness of his flesh.

The last droplets of the destroyed sword struck the tiles and hissed out. But not before Brak had glimpsed the damning evidence again:

Ool's left wrist did bear the mark Brak thought he had seen when the wind blew back the wizard's sleeves in the chariot—

The mark was a scarred ridge of tissue circling the left wrist. Once the man's flesh had been bound by a tight bracelet.

"You have come to perish, then," smiled Ool. "I shan't disappoint you—"

Immense, invisible hands created with no more than a blink of Ool's basilisk eyes lifted Brak and hurled him to the floor. His ears rang as he hit. His body went numb with pain.

Slowly the pale wizard advanced toward the place where the big barbarian lay writhing, trying to regather his strength. With a little purse of his lips Ool lifted one bare foot and placed it on Brak's sweating

chest. With his right hand he made a quick mesmeric pass.

Instantly Brak felt as though the weight of a building pressed down on him. He clenched his teeth, lashed his head from side to side, growled savagely—

But he could not move. He was held by the magical weight of Ool's soft, clammy foot.

From where he sprawled, Brak saw the magician's obscenely white face shine in the glare from behind the far curtain. Ool the sexless one lifted his left forearm, displayed the scarred wrist almost mockingly.

"Is this what you came to see, outlander? Well—" An exquisite shrug. "Look your last."

8

Brak the barbarian lay helpless under that pasty white foot, his arms and legs and trunk tingling faintly. The pain of his hard fall was diminishing. But he was still unable to move. He was prisoned not by visible weight but by the weight of Ool's arcane talents.

From what Brak could see of Ool whenever the white light source flared behind the distant curtain, the wizard continued to act amused. At length he gave voice to that amusement:

"You played boldly before my Lord Magnus, that I'll put to your credit. But you were foredoomed. Consider it an act of mercy on my part when I suggested you be allowed only two days and nights to work your nonexistent magic. No one can draw down the rain because I have gathered and held it. There."

A supple, almost boneless gesture with the left hand toward the rumbling light source.

"For the Children of the Smoke," Brak gasped out.

"Ultimately," Ool agreed. "But, in chief, for myself. You see—" The whitish lip hardened into a cruel line. "—years ago the Worldbreaker took something from me that represented unredeemable loss. Not by his own hand did he take it from me. But the hand which did the deed was his instrument. So I fled west to the lands of Shend, and for several years I discipled myself to their great wizards. I had some natural talent, I discovered—most humans do. Perhaps even you. But such talents lie dormant for lack of training and development. Had I not been so blessed, however, I would have sought another means of taking my revenge. In any case, when my preparations were complete, I returned to his court as a different man. Unrecognized. My plan was to gain the confidence of Lord Magnus. Thus I served him well and faithfully for years—"

"Until the time when you were ready to strike against him."

Ool nodded. "You have a sharper wit than the few northlanders I've encountered. You have brains you put to use—guessing, puzzling out answers—yes, you're right. I waited. Always maintaining secret communication with the Children. Always urging *them* to wait until their numbers were great enough—and Lord Magnus was old, his powers failing. The hour came finally, as I knew it would," Ool said with another purse of the moist lips. "In a few weeks—a month or two—but soon, the Children will sweep out of the east. By then, the maddened people within these walls will have no more heart or strength to resist. Even the army will rise, I imagine. Such is the miraculous power of nature's rain—and the lack thereof."

"Was—" Brak thrashed again. But the supernatural weight seemed to restrain every part of him. "—was it you then, who blacked the sky and filled the crystal idols with what looked like blood?"

"Of course," Ool smiled. "There will be additional—ah—demonstrations of that sort before I send my last signal to the Children. Alas, you spoiled that particular illusion. The blow from your chain, I think. Breaking the idol, it broke the projective trance. I was lying yonder—" He indicated the rumpled bedclothes that exuded a sweet but somehow foul perfume. "—arranging it all with my mind. Of a sudden I was jolted awake. Much the same thing happened when you killed my dear little guards. But enough of that. Although you are the loser and I am the winner in this small contest—"

He smiled again, seeing the glare in Brak's eyes. Again the big barbarian tried to move; futile. The naked foot held him. He could do nothing but clench and unclench his fists.

"—I respect certain of your qualities. I would like to know this much. What brought you here? These rooms are forbidden, even to the lord. I made sure of that long ago, so I could pursue my—private ventures undisturbed."

"The sight of the scar brought me," Brak said. "And certain things repeated by Captain Xeraph—"

Ool's hairless brows quirked, the back and sides of his oval head illuminated by another glare from behind the drape. "But when did you see the scar, pray? In public I keep my hands forever hid in full sleeves."

"I spied on your so-called spell-working at the water channel yesterday. While you were in the chariot, the wind blew your gown aside as the car went by the rocks where I was watching."

Ool was genuinely amused.

"I don't doubt your own people cast you out, my friend. No spell-worker of small talent could abide a man of your perceptions observing his mummery."

"But the holding back of the rain is no mummery—"

"I told you, I have not held it back," Ool corrected, crooking one pudgy finger in an almost schoolmasterish way. "I have imprisoned it. That, too, I learned in Shend, and thought it an excellent major weapon at the proper time. That time, mercifully, has come."

"Will—" Again Brak forced out each word. "Will you rule the Children when they take over the Worldbreaker's kingdom?"

After a thoughtful pause Ool replied, "I think not. I'll advise them, no doubt. Influence them. But the real savor of this victory will come long before I find myself in such a position." The white-oval face wrenched. "My only desire is to bring down that swilling, posturing little war cock!"

"At least—" Brak struggled to breathe. "—at least he'll die a man. Which is more than you can ever claim."

Ool's pale face contorted. He shrilled an almost feminine scream, leaning over. One wrathful hand slapped Brak's face. The blow was sharp, vicious. But the big barbarian hardly felt it; he felt something more important. Something for which he'd hoped and gambled with the gasped insult—

He felt the shift in weight on his chest. The pressure lessened ever so little. Still bent over, Ool was prey now. If he could strike fast enough—

Brak's chained hands came up. An inch. Another. Faster, *rising*—

By leaning to strike Brak's face, Ool had somehow weakened the occult weight. Brak could shift his trunk a little; raise one shoulder up in the same instant he seized Ool's left ankle with both hands, and wrenched.

Heaving against the phantom power holding him down, Brak managed to hurl the wizard off-balance. Ool toppled backward, linen wrap flying.

The wizard reeled into a taboret, collapsed it as he fell, floundering and shrieking. Brak struggled to his feet, his huge, rope-muscled body washed by the white glare from behind the drapery. The hollow boom rolled through the chamber as Brak drove himself toward that curtain and the secret it concealed—

Behind him Ool squealed and gibbered in rage. At any moment Brak expected some ensorcelled bolt of fire to strike him, char the flesh off his bones, burn him dead. His leaping strides were long, fear-driven—

Ool still flopped about on hands and knees, not yet fully recovered from his upsetting. Brak's hands closed on the white-shimmering drapery, coarse stuff. He tugged. Rings clattered. Fabric tore—

With a cry of terror Brak flung up an arm to shield his eyes.

On a low stone pedestal in an alcove stood a flask of strangely opalescent glass. The flask, stoppered, was no more than four hands high. Inside—*inside*—

Brak's skin crawled. His mouth tasted the bile of nauseous terror as he watched miniature storm clouds whirl and tumble within the flask.

The clouds moved with incredible speed, smashing the side of the glass prison, turning under and smashing again. Tiny lightning bolts sizzled and spat within the flask, spending themselves against the sides in unearthly fire showers—

As Ool had said: the storms of heaven; magically imprisoned.

Noise behind him. The wizard scrambling up—

Terrified almost witless, Brak grabbed at the awful flask, heard Ool shriek:

"Do not touch it—!"

The flask vibrated in Brak's hand, shooting off its white glare of prisoned lightnings, booming the sound of captured thunder. The flask cast a sickly white aura between the barbarian and the sorcerer, who was framed against the terrace where his dead guardians lay. Ool's supple white hands rose in the beginning of what Brak knew would be a last, death-bringing spell-cast—

He hurled the flask with all his strength.

Ool saw it flying at him, white and thundering. The

motions of his spell dissolved into frantic, fending gestures. He managed to hit the flask, deflect it. But when he saw the direction, he screamed and screamed—

The flask fell toward the floor.

Struck the tiles.

Shattered—

A cataclysm of light bursts and thunderclaps smote Brak's brain and body. Unleashed winds picked him up, tossed him toward the splitting ceiling, tumbled him and bounced him off a wall while noise drummed, glare burned, shrieking gale winds funneled skyward—

The whirlwind dropped Brak through white-glaring darkness, smashing the sense out of him an instant after he heard Ool's final scream drowned in the roar of furious, downpouring rain.

9

Bloodied, only half in possession of his senses, wracked with pain yet forcing himself to drag the flaccid white corpse by its ankle, Brak the barbarian sought the hall of Lord Magnus the Worldbreaker.

It was not hard to find. Drums hammered. Pipes skirled. Joyous, almost hysterical voices whooped and sang as he came limping up a long, empty corridor where torches blew and sheeting rain gusted in through high slot windows.

Staggering, Brak dropped to one knee. He released Ool's ankle, held both palms against his eyelids, fighting back the pain.

He had wakened in the apartment, finding half the ceiling caved away. The snapped end of a beam had crushed Ool's skull. Behind him, along the ghostly corridor, Brak could see a trail of red and gray paste where Ool's head had dragged.

For his part Brak had been prisoned beneath a rubble heap, badly knocked and gashed, but with no detectable damage besides general pain and a sharper one that might indicate a shattered bone somewhere in his left leg. He could barely support himself on that side.

Some of Ool's boy guardians had come creeping upstairs fearfully. At the sight of their dead master they fled into the night. Brak had pulled himself up and out of the ruins of the ceiling from which the prisoned storm forces had escaped to spread and deluge the land with the rain; rain that even now rivered loudly off the palace rooftop. He'd hauled Ool's shattered body through empty squares and courtyards while his pain-dulled mind perceived cries of jubilation from streets and palace buildings alike.

Now he gained his feet again. He saw a turning in the corridor just ahead. He clutched Ool's ankle, shambled on, drenched by a gust of rain through a window he passed. Cold, clean rain pouring down on the kingdom of Lord Magnus the Worldbreaker—

Weaving on his feet, struggling against the agony that seared his whole left side, Brak limped to the entrance of the huge hall, and waited.

A thousand people thronged there, it seemed, reveling. They axed open wine casks, lay beneath the pouring red streams, bathing in them. Others whooped and danced impromptu steps: soldiers and courtiers, ladies and serving maids alike—

One wine-drenched bawd saw Brak slouched in the great doorway and screamed.

The merrymaking ended. Heads turned. Mouths gaped.

Like some great wounded animal, Brak the barbarian dragged his victim on, up through a long, quickly opened aisle of faces to the foot of the beast-throne where Magnus the Worldbreaker sat, wine cup in hand.

The rain drummed and hammered in the dark night outside. Magnus' lined face bore a disbelieving look as he stared down at the grim, bloodied hulk of a man who, with his good right foot, rolled the wizard's corpse to the base of the throne stairs and then simply stared upward.

"Was it you who brought the rain—at the price of my wizard's life?" Magnus asked as if he couldn't quite countenance it. Ripples of amazement noised through the crowd, stilled suddenly by the lord's upraised hand.

At first Brak could manage no more than a single, pain-wracked shake of his head. Then he said:

"I only freed what your treacherous magician prisoned inside a flask with a powerful spell—to bring this kingdom down. Many—"

Brak saw three lords seated on the throne. Then two. He rubbed his eyes; fought the hurt spearing up his left side; stiffened his injured leg so he wouldn't totter and fall.

"—many years ago, I was told, a soldier ravished your wife and escaped. But not before a spear gave him a wound. Look at the wizard's arm, which he has kept concealed from you—from everyone—since the first day he came to your court. Once he wore your bracelet. Pull away his waist linen—" This Brak had already done, back in the apartment, to verify his suspicion. "A spear that struck in darkness robbed him of what a man can afford to lose least of all—"

He swayed, dizzy, as soldiers and courtiers ran forward to strip the corpse and expose the sexless, scarred ruin at the joining of Ool's pale legs.

A woman fainted. The linen was hastily replaced.

Lord Magnus gazed down in wonder and loathing. Brak forced out more hoarse words:

"He escaped to the land of Shend, and there learned sorceries. He returned and gained your favor under the name by which you knew him. For years he conspired with the Children of the Smoke, until the arrival of the hour he deemed opportune to—" A wracking cough that started deep in his belly nearly spilled Brak over. "—to bring you down. All this I will repeat in detail at—some better time." Glowering, he swung his head left and right. He missed the one face he sought: "Where is Captain Xeraph?"

"In the dungeons, being drawn on the wheel for permitting your escape."

"I struck him by surprise. He had no chance—let him go."

Silence.

"I said let him go!"

Lord Magnus signaled. Two senior officers dashed for a portal as Brak went on:

"Before I make my departure, I will explain fully how I destroyed the man who would have destroyed you, lord. But I want your leave—" Again a terrible, sick spell of dizziness swept him. The pain climbed through his left leg and his torso to eat at his brain. He braced his gashed left leg, dug horny nails into his palms: fresh pain, to sting his senses alive again.

"—to claim what you promised me if the rain came down in two days and two nights. That I will be free of your bondage."

Suddenly, horrifyingly, in the small, scarred face of Lord Magnus the Worldbreaker whose booted feet did not reach the floor in front of his throne, there was both cheerfulness and cunning. In the rain-hissing silence, the lord said:

"Barbarian, you heard me amiss. I spoke exactly this. *You will not die. You will not wear chains.* I never said you would go free. In fact I never intended that at all—and chose my words accordingly. I am ever in need of stout, quick-witted fighters—and will number you among such from this day forward. Instead of chains you will only wear the bronze bracelet of my army."

10

From somewhere deep in his hurt body Brak's cry of betrayal bellowed out:

"The gods damn you for deception—*I will escape!*"

Looking down on his new thrall with scarcely concealed admiration, Lord Magnus gave a tired, pleased nod.

"Accepted. I will prevent it, if I can."

It made no difference to Brak the barbarian that he knew why Lord Magnus had deceived him, and would impress him into service. In his terrible pain, he felt only hatred. Faces, forms, firelight from socketed torches swam together and melted into darkness as he threw his head back and let out one long, baying howl of animal rage.

Lunging, he tried to climb the throne stairs to his captor. But he was too weak. He fell back, sprawling over the corpse of Ool. His mind darkened swiftly—

There was sudden stillness except for the hammer of the rain. The unconscious barbarian's right arm slipped off the dead magician's shoulder where it had rested and struck the floor with a last faint clattering of chain.

THE MIRROR OF WIZARDRY

1

All through a cold and forlorn afternoon while the sleet slashed against his face, the big barbarian pushed his stolen pony higher toward the distant pass. He could no longer see the pass itself. Snowstorms ahead had obscured the craggy mountains through which it cut like a wound left in raw flesh by a dagger. But he kept moving, even though his teeth chattered from the cold and the exhaustion of six days on ponyback with precious little rest and even less food. Every league he traveled put him that much further away from the outriders of Lord Magnus.

"Keep going, lad," he told the tired pony. "This is no land to rest in. With luck, there'll be time and forage beyond the pass."

The pass represented his main chance. Once through it, he would cross a border and be outside the jurisdiction of the lord in whose army he had served, against his will, for nearly a year. Or so the old man whom he'd bribed three days ago had told him at a seedy caravanserai at which he'd stopped.

He had emptied his waist pouch of the last of his few dinshas to obtain that information. Like most of those under the heavy hand of Lord Magnus, the old man had been reluctant to speak of anything beyond the weather to a stranger. But having broken his silence for a price, he had babbled freely and had even drawn a rough map of the fastest route to the pass.

The map had served well enough at first. Now, as

he dug his knees into his weary pony and inclined his head to keep the sleet from his eyes, he wasn't sure that he hadn't been gulled by the toothless haggler. The land here didn't fit the map, and he had the nagging worry that he had become lost.

It was a lonely land.

Formidable and ugly, the mountains ringed him. Even when the sleet finally let up, sailing snowclouds hid the summit. Up there, the old man had told him, vicious storms made travel next to impossible at certain seasons. And this was supposed to be near the beginning of such a time.

In the east, as Brak had noted the day before, the peaks formed an almost uninterrupted rampart. According to tales told by soldiers in the army of Lord Magnus, the Mountains of Smoke hid the birthplace of the elder gods. What lay east of the mighty barrier few could say. None cared to speculate about it except with broadswords handy. The tales hinted at wizards and adepts at the forbidden arts of magic, and only a fool mentioned a wizard, lest his attention be called to the speaker.

Brak had crossed the treeline near noonday. Now he was climbing a twisting trail strewn with huge boulders. Before he reached the pass hidden by the brawling snowstorm ahead, he would be within the heart of the Mountains of Smoke. The prospect was forbidding, but the restless urge to freedom drove him on, coupled with his knowledge of what Lord Magnus' men would do if they caught up with him. He'd seen other deserters from the impressed army last for as long as a week before death finally relieved them of their agony.

Suddenly he heard a thin, keening sound over the

noise of the storm. It lasted a moment, died away, and then came again.

"Fever noise," the barbarian grunted. He knew he was ripe for disease from exposure or the bad water he'd been forced to drink. He pounded his palm against one near-frozen ear.

But the keening kept on, modulated by the wind. Again he slammed his hand against his head, hitting the other ear. Little ice crystals that had formed on the long yellow braid hanging down his back tinkled and fell off. The noise rose to a sudden shriek, and Brak realized that it was not a product of his own mind but the very real wail of another human being.

This was the last place he should expect to find a traveler, but the cry was now unmistakable. It could be no scout of Lord Magnus, however; the cry came from ahead of him.

He muttered to himself, knowing his own business was more urgent than his interest in another could be. Then he shrugged. "A little faster, lad," he growled to the laboring pony and dug his knees in harder.

The storm had been abating somewhat, but now a sudden flurry made vision difficult. He rounded another huge boulder, followed a tricky curve in the trail, guided his mount across a slippery crust of ice and approached a dimly seen opening ahead at fair speed.

The thin, poorly loomed cloak of gray belled from his shoulders, and his cheap tunic flapped around his waist, having worked loose from the garment of lion's hide at his hips. The braid of hair and the tail of the lion skin stood out behind him as he fought the pony up a rise and went into a skidding descent on an icy slope beyond.

The wind quieted suddenly, cut off by the rocks

around, and his vision suddenly improved. He saw a fairly spacious cuplike depression completely surrounded by rocky walls. At the far side of the hollow he made out a strange shape, leaping and seeming to flap wildly. His ears filled with the frightened cries of a human voice. Now he could hear a weird oddly terrifying snapping and clicking from nearby. There was nothing human about those sounds.

He clutched at the hilt of his huge broadsword with one hand while the other dragged back on the reins of the frightened pony. As the pony came to a skidding stop, he could see the flapping apparition was a woman.

She was running in frantic zigzag course between peculiar round boulders that seemed to be strewn across the floor of the depression. Her arms were waving frantically to balance her twisting body, and her hair trailed out behind her. As she ran, she screamed.

As Brak sent the pony charging toward her, the clicking sound seemed to multiply suddenly. *Clicka-clack, clicka-clack!* Abruptly the pony whinnied in fear and shied.

Brak looked down and shock jolted through him.

One of the small brown stones suddenly split horizontally across its blank face. The edges of the crack widened, and a rocky maw gaped, widely, edged with sharp rock crystals like teeth.

Brak had seen enough things in his travels to make him reasonably immune to the usual frights and wonders. But he had never seen a living stone opening to bite with savage crystal fangs!

The pony stumbled on a patch of ice. Too late, Brak shifted his weight to avert the disaster. The pony's forefoot slid close to the widening maw of living rock. There was a ghastly snapping of crystal teeth as the rock bit together, and the pony's hoof sheared off, spouting blood. The animal screamed and reared.

Brak tumbled frantically to the left, barely pulling himself free. He fell with jarring force, still gripping the broadsword in his hand. When he could look again, he saw the pony floundering on its side. And from all directions the strange rocks were converging. They rolled toward the struggling animal with little side-to-side motions. Jaws were opening and clicking shut in each rock.

As Brak started for the pony, he heard the woman scream again. He turned his head, and it nearly proved his undoing. He felt something move against his foot; he leaped back, just before one of the rocks snapped its hideous jaws together where his ankle had been.

He jerked backward several quick steps. The rolling rocks were gathered around the fallen pony, and the jaws were articulating wildly, clashing and biting. The pony squealed, and blood was flowing from a dozen wounds.

Howling with rage, Brak plunged forward. He jumped over three of the stones that gnashed at him. He drove his broadsword through the neck of the pony and deeper toward its brain. The animal gave a shudder and mercifully went limp.

Small savage teeth raked against the hard leather that encased Brak's heel. He whirled as the jaws of stone started to shut on his boot. He thrust downward with his sword, ramming the iron savagely into the rock jaws. The rock was porous and soft, like pumice, and the broadsword sheared through it. The rock rolled backward as it split, the jaws clashing harshly.

As the sword came free, a vile smelling jet of yellow

gas poured from between the stone teeth. That rock lay quiet, but all around the other rocks rolled and crunched toward him, bumping against and over the dead pony, and closing in.

2

His face contorted with anger, Brak jumped as high and far as he could, to land on bent knees a short distance beyond the clacking stones. He dodged the nearest one and turned toward the place where he had last seen the woman.

She had fallen chest down into a channel of trickling water that ran through the depression. Her fall had broken a thin crust of ice, and she lay with one leg twisted beneath her, her peasant robe soaking up water. She seemed to be breathing but was unconscious. A dozen rocks were rolling toward her from all directions. As he ran, Brak glimpsed another fallen horse. It was little more than bones and blood. More of the stones were clustered around and on top of it, and the sounds of the rock jaws crunching was a loud cacophony. Brak ran faster.

A rock rolled down to the water's edge, near the woman's outstretched foot. Brak brought his broadsword down. The stone seemed to sense the attack and hitched itself sideways. His blade glanced off it with a ringing clang.

The force of his charge and the icy ground sent one foot out from under him, and he fell to one knee. Instantly more of the stones at the water's edge converged on him.

As he forced himself up from the icy water, he switched his grip so that both hands were around the hilt of the broadsword. Then, yelling the guttural oaths of the high steppes, the wild lands of the north where he'd been born, he hacked and chopped and bludgeoned until the depression rang with the clamor of iron and the harsher sound of breaking rocks.

Darkness was beginning to fall, cutting down his range of vision. Still the rocks rolled forward, and Brak still hacked, gouged, and slashed. Rage was like a cloud of red mist across his eyes.

He had come to see that the rocks could not enter the moving water, but he did not retreat the foot or so that would carry him beyond their reach. Instead he moved out of the stream, carrying the fight to them.

Finally, thews aching and belly heaving, he let the broadsword drop. He scraped both sides on the bank of the little stream, looking for damage to the blade. There were scratches, but it was still a usable weapon. Then he wiped the ice crystals from his eyes and stared through the gloom.

The horse and his pony were piles of white bones. The rocks, sated or driven off by his furious attack, were in full retreat. Their stone jaws were almost silent now. He watched the last rock bump out of sight toward the depression walls, now almost hidden in darkness and the snow that was beginning to fall.

He stared down at the immobile rocks that surrounded him. They were no longer moving, their split roundness showing no sign of gaping maws. It was impossible to tell that they had ever been anything but what they now seemed. He shuddered and drew breath deeply into his lungs. Then he heard a faint sound.

The woman was conscious again.

She lay on her side in the trickling water, watching him. An arm that had been moving when he first saw her stilled quickly as she saw his gaze. He tried to smile at her, though his face felt frozen. But she didn't respond. She was obviously terrified at the sight of him.

There was still enough light for him to see that she had fair hair and a pleasing form that even her soaked and bedraggled cloak could not hide. She had an olive face with the hint of southern climes in the dark eyes; it should have been pretty, but now it was haggard and fear-stricken.

Brak lumbered toward her, holding out his hand. She stared wide-eyed at his big fingers.

"My pony is dead and so is your horse," he said. "We need to find a shelter."

Automatically he glanced toward the pile of bones that had been his pony, heartsick at the loss. It had been his only friend for days, as well as his only means of swift passage through the Mountains of Smoke.

But now the girl claimed his attention. She was obviously on the edge of screaming terror. He tried to soften his voice as he extended his hand clumsily again. "Come, girl, I won't harm you."

"Garr sent you!" Her teeth rattled with more than cold as she drew back from him. "You're with Lord Garr—or the wizard, Valonicus! I know you are!"

"I'm with none but you," he said, annoyed. "Will you get up before we both freeze?"

When she wouldn't, he slammed his broadsword back in place and stooped to pick her up. At first, she protested. But when he flung her unceremoniously over his shoulder, she gave up the struggle.

Double-damned and triple-damned luck, he thought as he plodded up the trail in the darkening snow. Pony gone and burdened with a woman half out of her mind and ranting of wizards. It seemed that the elder gods who reputedly inhabited these regions at the eastern limit of the known world mocked him indeed, and bid him fail in his flight toward freedom and the open highroads.

Then he frowned, thinking of her words again. Maybe there was more than mere ranting of a wizard in her accusation—maybe she knew more than he'd first thought. Brak had heard legends of the ancient days when the elementals of earth were overcome by the elder gods and chained in rocks, forbidden to exercise their evil craving for the blood of life. It was said that a wizard could unchain them for a day by powerful spells, though no wizard Brak had seen could do the trick.

But what wizard could unleash their evil from untold distance? And if such a wizard did exist, what had Brak got himself into?

Warily now he climbed higher through the storm. As night fell fully, he found a cave. It offered shelter to his body but scant comfort to his mind.

3

Brak still had a few dried lumps of meat in his pouch. These he shared with the girl. She munched in silence, eyeing him with huge opal eyes full of terror.

He'd managed to gather a bundle of small sticks from the stunted shrubs that grew above the tree line, and the back of the little cave had a nest of old rubble from occupancy by some animal. They gave off an unpleasant odor after he pulled them in a corner of the cave and struck them to fire, but they took the chill off the damp place. Now he squatted across from the girl as the flames threw shifting patterns across her wind-chapped skin.

She wasn't more than twenty years old, he judged, though her nerves and a touch of hardness about her made her seem older. She started at every sound from outside and seemed to be listening when there was no sound.

"Better get out of those wet clothes," he advised.

She finished the last of her meat. "No." Terror darted into her eyes. *"No!"*

He shrugged. "Be stubborn, then. But you're a fool. I've no desire to molest you. Not in this cold."

His crude grin meant to reassure her, but it won no warming response. She said, as if it were explanation enough: "You're a barbarian!"

"So they say. My name is Brak, by the way."

Hoping to put her at ease, he began telling her about himself from his birth in the high steppes to his desire to seek his fortune in the warm climes of Khurdisan far to the south. He held out his huge arm to show the scabs at his wrist where the smith had been bribed to hack away the bronze bracelet that all soldiers of Lord Magnus wore.

"So it took a year to get free of his army, but here I am—wherever here is," he finished. He crossed his legs and tried to smile again. "Now, what about you?"

After a brief hesitation she nodded. "My name is Nari."

"That's a start. Where do you come from?"

Memory cast an ugly veil over her beauty. "From the kingdom of Gilgamarch, many leagues to the west."

"I've heard of Gilgamarch in my travels, though I've never been there."

She clasped her hands around her legs protectively. Another chill seized her. The small fire had done little to dry her sodden garments. "Better that you haven't. It's a kingdom of filthy men who would—do anything to—"

She stopped, but he urged her on. "What brought you here to those fanged rocks?"

She shuddered, her face paling a trifle. "Gods! My horse fell before I knew—and they were closing around me—" She covered her face with her hands in a gesture that was somehow contrived and calculated.

Brak waited for the horror of her memories to pass. Then, more firmly than before, he said, "Nari, I'm the owner of a fairly even temper—except when I'm done an injustice. This evading my questions *is* an injustice. At least you owe me some explanation of what one lone girl is doing in the Mountains of Smoke. You know why I'm here—running toward the pass and a road south." His eyes hardened as he waited. "Tell me, Nari."

"I'm running at well," she whispered.

"From the wizard you mentioned?" Brak asked. "The one who can free the stone demons without even being here?"

"Valonicus," she said. "And he could have been here, since he can travel without his body." She shuddered, then shook her head. "No, I'm fleeing from Garr, who calls himself Lord of Gilgamarch. He's only the illegitimate half brother of the rightful lord who sits on the throne, but he's a year older and claims his right of precedence. And Valonicus serves him, for some reason I do not know. I came to the Mountains of Smoke with them because I believed Garr."

Suddenly there was a new, angry note in her voice. She edged forward toward the fire, her face intense.

"I have a secret, barbarian—one that was given me as a child. Through years of poverty—living in hovels, one step ahead of the slavers—I saved that secret. Then Garr appeared, planning to seize the throne. And I offered him that secret in return for his pledge that I should sit on the throne as queen when he won. So I rode here with him and Valonicus, who could bring forth the marks my father—"

She stopped abruptly, then went on too quickly. "Garr's a fool. I had the secret that could win him the army to take the throne. But he lied to me. I sneaked back when he thought me gone ahead and heard him plotting with Valonicus, laughing at the gutter girl who wanted to be queen. So I fled at night before the secret was fully revealed, up the trail ahead of him."

There was a flash of something strange in her eyes. Brak considered it, his hand unconsciously reaching toward the great broadsword. "Then this Lord Garr and the wizard may be following you now for the secret—and close behind?"

Terror mounted in the dark eyes again. "Yes."

He swore softly to himself for wasting time in idle talk. Then he grimaced. In this storm and without a horse there was little enough he could have done. "How many fighting men with them?"

"Three. Ruffians and murderers who have fled the army."

Five men—and one of them a wizard—against a single unmounted fighter made the odds too long. Unless the girl was lying. "This secret they're chasing you for—what is it, Nari?"

Suspicion washed over her face. "The price is a throne, barbarian. You don't need it."

Brak cursed again to himself but gave up. Her answer could be from ambition or the action of a romantic girl lying to make herself more than she was. He fished the last sliver of meat from near the fire and munched it. Then he rose and stretched.

"Very well. You'd better sleep. But first take off those wet robes and dry them. Wear this while you do." He unloosed his gray cloak and flung it to her.

She started to shake her head. A couple of drops of melted ice fell from her fair hair onto her hand, and she stared at them. At length she gave a meek, tired nod.

"All right. But you must go outside."

"As you wish." The modesty seemed false in her, somehow, but he was in no mood to argue further. "Don't flatter yourself that it's a great sacrifice to me, though."

The lion tail swung behind him as he stalked out

into the night. He wandered a short way down the rock slope, sucking in the painfully cold night air. For the moment, at least, the storm had passed and the sky was mostly clear, though cloud masses still threatened near the horizon. The deep dark of winter formed a black bowl up above, relieved only by the thin sliver of the moon and here and there the sharp light of the brighter stars.

She was probably telling the truth as she saw it, he decided. The biting rocks must have been meant as a trap, and hardly for him. So there was a mighty wizard somewhere behind, and a usurping lord. It was a bad combination to cross. The prospects seemed even more gloomy than they had an hour ago.

Brak stared up past the dim cave mouth toward the east. There, summits still hidden by clouds of drifting snow, the Mountains of Smoke reared bleak and forbidding. He thought he could pick out the darker gap of the pass that was his destination. Apparently the old man's map had been right, after all.

To the left of it, in an area previously hidden by the storm, he noticed a strange black rock formation. It contrasted sharply with the vast white patches of glacial ice around it. By uncertain moonlight the black formation seemed to resemble the skull of a man.

Or was it only his imagination brewing phantasms and omens out of shadows? He shivered again. After what he judged was time enough for the girl to change, he turned and climbed back toward the cave entrance.

He must have misjudged the time, or she had dawdled. Nari was still busy spreading her soaked garments out to dry by the fire and her naked back was toward him. It was a shapely back, and Brak's eyes rested on it with normal male approval at first. Then eyes flared wide as he stood in the shadows and looked at what lay on the olive skin revealed in the firelight. He was still staring when she reached down gracefully and raised his cloak. She swirled it around her shoulders, hiding her flesh.

Quickly Brak retreated a few steps, coughed, and rattled stones with his foot. Then he marched up and into the cave.

Nari huddled against the cave wall, watching him with alert eyes.

"It's bitterly cold out there, but I heard no horsemen," he told her. "Perhaps the lord and wizard have turned back."

"No." She was positive. "They will find me. And hearing no sounds of horses from far off means nothing. Valonicus has other means of traveling, as I told you. His mirror—"

Again she stopped.

"Damn, girl, can't you finish anything? Your obscure hints would make any man angry."

For the first time she seemed genuinely concerned. "I'm sorry, Brak. Garr and many others have used me badly, and it leaves a mark, though I don't mean to sound distrustful. I thank you for what you did in the place of rocks. But I can best thank you for that by not making you share the secret that has put Garr and Valonicus on my trail." She smiled wearily. "May I sleep now?"

"Sleep," he told her. "Good night."

He picked up his sword again and went to stand guard by the cave entrance. His eyes roved from the far stars to what he could see of the trail, and his thoughts narrowed to the mystery of the girl who was already asleep behind him.

From the base of her neck to the midpoint of her spine her back had been covered with strange markings and colorations, all arranged in a curiously tantalizing design which was meaningless except for one detail. They had ended in obvious lack of completion, as if half of the drawing was still to be shown.

One thing had been clear enough, however. Between her shoulder blades there was a black configuration that resembled the skull-rock up by the pass. It resembled the thing so closely that even now Brak's palms itched at the felt presence of some dark and unknown menace.

Some of the menace was clear enough, however. If her half-revealed secret lay on her back and that involved the skull-rock formation by the pass, they were in for trouble. Garr and Valonicus would be bound for a destination that matched the route he had to take.

4

Many hours later, after the moon had set, weariness finally overcame the big barbarian. He abandoned his useless watch and lay down near the mouth of the cave. The fire had burned almost out; little remained but small coals that shone like orange gems. Brak could barely see Nari's huddled form. Her breathing was light and restless, as though nightmares troubled her. Now and then she moaned. He listened to the night stillness. There was no sound of hooves or the sound of men. The cold iron of his broadsword rested against his bare leg, and he curled his fingers around the hilt.

The cheap tunic did little to protect him against the biting cold, but he had grown up with such hardships. In time he slept in utter exhaustion. He never knew afterward how long he dozed before the gray light wakened him.

It could not have been long. Total darkness still gripped the world outside the cave. Brak swam up from slumber, grunting in annoyance at the pale radiance that flickered against his closed eyelids. Now it waned, then it waxed. He opened his eyes, to choke back a cry of dismay and shock.

A radiant gray cloud whirled in the cave mouth. Through it Brak could see the far stars, though they were indistinct and discolored. The cloud spun around and around with a deep whistling sound.

Then its grayness brightened to a white and grew in brilliance until it lit all the cave's interior and

brought Nari out of her slumber with a thick, low cry.

Brak's hand was suddenly sweat-slimed, and he rubbed it against his tunic before taking a firmer grip on the sword hilt. He bent his right leg beneath him, preparing to rise and confront whatever the light might be. But before he could come to his feet, he saw that the blazing cloud was rearranging itself into the pattern of a human figure.

The man-shaped cloud hovered just above the ground. Its hands were hidden in the voluminous sleeves of a robe that was marked with cabalistic symbols. The head of the figure was abnormally large and completely hairless, looking like a skull; below the bald pate was a triangular face, and the phantom's pronounced cheekbones and bony brow ridges lent the face a mad, fantastic cast. From above a fierce-chiseled nose, two oval eyes watched and searched. In all the whiteness of the apparition, the only color belonged to the eyes, which were a brilliant yellow.

Behind Brak, in the darkness, Nari screamed.

The specter-lips cracked and smiled as Brak stumbled to his feet with sword arm drawn back. He stepped forward cautiously, then advanced another step. The cloud began to disintegrate. The features of the phantom face melted, returning to wisps of smoke.

Nari's shrieking beat against the big barbarian's ears as he forced himself to move. The yellow eyes glared from one of them to the other. Dimly Brak understood that he and the girl had been seen and recognized. The eyes of the specter broke apart and drained of color.

Brak howled savagely and ran at the horror with his broadsword.

As he drove the point of his weapon into the cloud,

its whirling motion seemed to cease for the length of a heartbeat. Some shocking force jolted back through the blade into Brak's hand and ran up his wrist and arm. He was hurled from his feet and thrown against the wall of the cave, still clutching the sword. The tip of the weapon struck against the rock with a wild clangor.

Immediately the process of dissolution began again, and the cloud faded. The whistling sound died away, and the thing was gone.

Brak blinked his eyes and shook his head, muttering a curse. His backbone crawled as he came to his feet, and his arm still seemed numb from the jolt he had received.

By some eldritch means whatever thing had been in the cloud had suspended its disappearance long enough to demonstrate its power with the blast of agony through Brak's sword. The eyes in the thing had looked on his attack as effrontery, and it had shown its contempt and wrath deliberately.

Now even the cloud of fine ash that had been stirred from the fire began to settle. Brak could see nothing but the bleak vista of the mountains outside the cave, with a hint of false dawn breaking.

He lumbered back to where Nari rocked back and forth on her haunches. She was sobbing uncontrollably, and he struck her face with the flat of his hand. She cried out at the blow, but the punishment had the desired effect. She calmed slowly and began to release herself from the tight ball in which she had been.

Brak gripped her shoulders between his huge hands. "You recognized that hell-thing. Your scream said as much. Well?"

She gulped and tried to speak, but only meaningless

noise came from her lips. Then she caught herself and nodded tightly. "It was Valonicus. It was the wizard."

"But not the real wizard. What was it—his ghost sent out to spy on us?"

Nari wiped tears from her cheeks. "No, not his ghost. At least he stays aware while he sends it out. He can make a duplicate of himself—create another wizard of smoke." Her shoulders wrenched and she shuddered. "I've seen him perform the trick for Garr when the trail was hard to follow and he wanted to scout our way. He can send the shadow-self traveling at great distances."

Brak grunted. "So I think you hinted before. And I suppose he used the shadow to free the rock demons, though how a shadow of light can cast a spell . . . What kind of mirror is it?"

"It looks like any mirror, despite the enchantment, though the glass shines on both sides. It's mounted in spindles at the top and bottom so he can twirl it. Valonicus always keeps it on his person and allows no one else to touch it."

"I've heard of seeing through magic mirrors but not sending out ghosts through them," Brak said. "But the thing was alive and aware. It watched us."

She nodded. "And Valonicus knows what it saw, Valonicus is an evil man, but they say he's the greatest of all sorcerers. Garr doles out what little wealth he still has in his coffers to keep the wizard with him. He has promised that Valonicus will be the supreme head of the priestly cult in Gilgamarch after the army he raises can take the throne. From the talk I heard at the campfires, Valonicus had been thrown out of many other countries, and he's willing to do anything for Garr in return for a place of power of his own."

"Still, he's a fool," Brak said, voicing thoughts that had been in the back of his mind. "He wants you alive for your secret, but he sets the rock demons against you. That makes no sense."

She shook her head. "The rocks attacked the horses and you. But now that I've had time to think, I remember they never actually touched me. They were only partly freed."

Suddenly Nari's control broke, and she thrust herself against Brak's broad chest. Convulsions shook her whole body. He touched her hair gently and tried as best he could to comfort her. The dawn must be breaking, since there was light enough now for Brak to see fear lurking deep in the girl's eyes.

She pushed herself away with a final shiver. "Now that Valonicus has sent his ghostly double to discover us, he and Lord Garr will soon be here. They'll double their speed to catch us."

With a nod of bleak agreement, Brak replied, "Then we must double ours as we flee them."

"Where?"

"To the pass that leads from the Mountains of Smoke," he answered. It went where he had to go, and it was no worse a choice for escape from Garr and Valonicus than any other.

"It's useless, Brak. We can't travel fast enough to outrun them," she protested.

He knew she was probably right, but it was no reason to give up now. He grinned at her without humor. "We can try."

She nodded reluctantly. He left the cave while she put on her own clothing. Then, bundled again in his cloak, he led the way along the rocky trail that wound upward around the side of the slope. The summits of the peaks hid behind windblown clouds of snow. A storm was again rising, and he grumbled at the weather that seesawed without reason here.

Ahead, through a rent in the clouds, Brak glimpsed the black skull-rock.

5

The wind rose as they went on, and Brak bent into it, already frozen to the center of his bones by its blast. Nari stumbled often, leaning on him for support as they wended their way higher.

Brak moved on steadily, but his mind was only half on their progress. The memory of the black skull-rock and the similar shape on her back bedeviled the curiosity that was always strong in him; and the picture of the yellow eyes out of the cloud stayed in his thoughts making his belly churn with alarm.

Snow began to slant through the air around them. Fat flakes drifted against their cheeks and onto their eyebrows. The wind sang like a lonely ghost and blew the snow in cold veils.

They slipped and stumbled often. Brak's calves ran with blood where he gouged them on rocky outcroppings, and he was for once grateful for the stout leather Lord Magnus had used for his mounted soldier's boots. The trail became choked with snow, and following it grew harder. The sun dimmed from a disc to a vague opalescent light that shed no warmth.

Finally, after what seemed like hours of tramping and with no certainty that they were any closer to their destination than when they started, Brak called a halt.

They rested in the lee of a boulder, out of the chilling wind. He sat down in the damp snow and wrapped his cloak around them both. Nari's teeth were chattering, and she huddled against him.

"We'll never live to reach the pass, barbarian."

"I faced worse blizzards when I was a youngster. It's certain our chances will be even worse if we allow your Lord Garr and his sorcerer to catch us."

"They would kill you," she agreed. Then she added, without relief. "They wouldn't *kill* me."

"Encouraging thought," he mumbled. "How so?"

"Because the treasure map on the skin of my back is only half complete and once I'm dead, Valonicus couldn't—"

Suddenly she closed her mouth as she realized that her fatigue had betrayed her. Snow drifted against her eyelids as she stared up at the barbarian's face. She pulled away, again afraid of him.

"Treasure," he said. It fitted. A usurper always needed more money than he could get to make his dreams of raising an army come true.

"I didn't mean . . . I don't know what I'm saying, Brak."

Again she stopped as she saw the hardening of his mouth.

But his voice was as patient as he could make it. "Nari, we're both playing poor odds with death. The time for your games is done. I want to know what I'm protecting you from and why. Why are Garr and his wizard after you? You can tell me or not—but if not, I'll head for the pass without you to slow my way."

She huddled back against him, seeming almost relieved as she answered him.

Her father had been a magician of some note himself, and his name—Krim Shan—was respected in the court of the Yellow Emperors of Tobool far to the west. Ten years earlier he had accompanied the son of the emperor, Lord Yian, a venturesome young man, on a treasure expedition over the crest of the Mountains of Smoke.

The young prince proved right, and instead of a precipice where the world ended or a belching hell in which the nestling gods were raised, the expedition found a wealthy mountain kingdom ripe for plundering. Lord Yian's soldiers stripped the kingdom of vast stores of precious metal and bulging chests full of priceless gems.

But a magician of the kingdom had cursed them mightily before he died and the party met with disaster in returning through the Mountains of Smoke. A storm of enormous proportions killed Lord Yian and most of his companions in a series of cataclysmic avalanches. Krim Shan and three others escaped with their lives. The treasure was lost down a crevasse that opened at the height of the avalanche.

They had no means to reclaim the treasure, and their lives would be forfeit if they returned to announce that the prince had died. They decided to seek safety in Gilgamarch, stopping so that Krim Shan could send a trusted friend to spirit away his daughter and bring her to him. On the journey south the three died, and Krim Shan was stricken with a fatal plague. He died the sole man possessing knowledge of the location of the lost treasure of Tobool.

But before he died, he reached Gilgamarch with his only heir, Nari. At that time she was but eight years old. Breathing his last in a filthy hovel in the stews of the capital, he summoned his magicial powers and traced in the flesh of the young girl's back a detailed map to the treasure.

Then, with a special unguent, he made the map

vanish until the time when a proper counter potion could be applied. He called for a scroll and stylus and with these wrote his legacy. He thrust it into the hands of the sobbing child and expired.

Nari grew up to gradual realization of the value of her father's gift. The scroll told her that any qualified sorcerer could bring the map forth on her skin by the use of the proper hot applications of available herbs.

Brak nodded as she stopped her tale. "And you bided your time, waiting for the right person to whom you could barter the secret. Didn't you ever think of trying to reclaim the treasure yourself, instead of offering it to another?"

"At first," she told him. "But I had no money for an expedition, nor could a woman head it. Brak, as a child I ran wild and hungry in the streets, begging for crusts to stay alive. I began dreaming of wealth, but in time I wanted more. I wanted protection and a man who could make me respectable."

Her mouth twisted as she continued. "Finally I heard of Lord Garr. I went to him, and we struck a bargain—my body with the map in return for a throne." She shook her head. "I was a fool to think a man like that could respect me. But at least I escaped and destroyed the wizard's potion before the map could be completed. He's not happy now, the proud and unfaithful dog!"

"Then why should he want you, if he can't restore the map?" Brak asked.

She huddled closer, and the temper died out of her. "I was more fool than I said, Brak. The wizard knows another way to bring out the map. And that—"

Brak considered it silently. It accounted for the

black skull-rock between her shoulders—a marker that could not be missed. It seemed to fit what he had seen on her back and explain why the markings had been incomplete. Maybe with luck . . .

"Could the two of us take the treasure if we found it?"

"I don't think so. It will still be buried in the crevasse. Garr's men brought pack animals laden with special tools and ropes for getting down and digging through the ice. He expected to send back to Gilgamarch for more help after he dug up enough to pay for supplies and men."

"Then we'd best ignore it," Brak decided. He rose, brushing the snow away from his eyes. "Time to move for the pass. We have rested enough."

With a weary sigh Nari got to her feet. The snow came up around their ankles, now crusting and numbing. The girl's expression was forlorn as they set out.

"My father meant to leave me a treasure of great price," she remarked bitterly. "Now it has become nothing but a curse. If we escape, barbarian, I'll make my life different. I'll save my secret until I've lived together with a man long enough to know him well. Brak, what's wrong?"

Brak's hand was raised in warning. Out in the snow he heard a clink of pony harness. He guided Nari to the left through the drifts, while his hand dropped to the hilt of his broadsword. Suddenly a horse's head loomed out of the storm, and a cowled face stared at them with eyes of deep yellow.

"Lord Garr!" the horseman cried. "We've run them to earth!"

6

Hooves spun the snow away in white streamers. Four riders charged out of the murk behind the gray-robed horseman who kneed his stallion to one side to let the others pass. Brak flung Nari behind him and freed his sword, snarling at the foes who faced him.

The four riders wore dark cloaks and heavy leather helms and breastplates. Carved half-moon blades flashed in their hands. They galloped up around Brak, hemming him in between the heaving flanks of their mounts. He raised his broadsword, but they were no fools; they kept at a distance just out of his reach, but where one could ride at him instantly. One of the riders, taller and with heavy snow-rimed mustaches, uttered a harsh laugh and flicked the ornamented reins of his bridle. "So this is the outlander you saw, Valonicus?"

"Run, girl!" Brak howled and leaped to attack.

His broadsword swung, but the shout had given warning to the rider, and the blade glanced off the breastplate of the moving man. At the same time the rider hacked down with his scimitar. Brak dodged. The blade whistled past his ear, barely missing him.

The rider hacked again, and this time he nipped a bit of skin from Brak's cheek. Bleeding, the big barbarian leaped high and drove his sword into the man's chest with all the force of both his arms. The rider shrieked and tumbled from the saddle, dragging the broadsword with him.

The tall man with the mustaches was shouting orders, and the two other riders flung themselves out of their wooden saddles to leap on Brak's back. The suddenness of their move caught him off-balance, and he went down on his hands and knees, while they pounded him with blows from their fists and boots.

He shook his head dizzily and started to struggle to his feet, but it was too late. A rider stood near him with ready scimitar. The other had found Brak's gory broadsword and now pitched it off into the snow, where it vanished into a drift. Brak heard Nari screaming and searched for her in the blowing white confusion of the storm. He saw her staggering away, but too close for any hope of escape.

The cowled wizard Valonicus rode after her. He caught her, wrapped his long-nailed hand in her hair, and jerked her to a stop. His yellow eyes were dancing with evil humor as he dragged her back to where the two soldiers were guarding Brak.

Garr brushed some flecks of snow from his mustaches and dismounted now, making a show of elegance in his manner. He had a mottled red face and one of his eyes looked milky in the pupil. Yet there was a power about him, a certain air of assurance as he stalked up to Brak and flicked the barbarian across the face with a soft leather glove.

"Has Nari told you her pitiful tale, outlander? Has she gulled you into trying to help her?"

Brak glared back without answering.

Garr's cheeks became more mottled. "Valonicus, this long-haired lout shows a lack of respect to the Lord of Gilgamarch."

Valonicus threw Nari down in the snow and climbed leisurely down from his horse. His hands were hidden in the voluminous sleeves of his symbol-marked robe, just as they had been when the smoke-double appeared in the cave. Brak recognized the face, and a crawling shudder worked down his back. The gaze of the wizard was cruel and sure, now tinged with some vile mirth.

"Lord Garr!" Brak shouted. "Strumpet's son, you mean!"

One of the soldiers kicked him in the groin, doubling him over in agony. Garr let out a pleased laugh.

"Before we kill him or leave him to die, Valonicus, can't you give him some instructions in the art of being respectful to his betters?"

"A most seemly suggestion," the wizard answered. "It will give us time to get the kinks of too much riding out of our muscles."

Garr turned back to Brak, and he was smiling now. "Crawl for me, barbarian," he suggested softly. "Crawl on your hands and knees and do me homage."

Snarling, Brak lunged for him, to be brought up short by the grip of two soldiers. Valonicus made a swift, supple gesture of tossing something invisible at Brak and muttered a string of singsong words.

For a moment nothing seemed to happen, and Brak drew a breath of relief. Then some ghastly force seemed to reach out an unseen hand and seize all of his limbs at once. Before he could try to resist, he was smashed flat on his chest in the snow.

His vision blurred as he fought the devil's force that seemed to constrict around his body. He found his knees bending and his torso sliding forward. His hands scrabbled in the snow, lifting him so that he found himself on his hands and knees before Garr.

Even his neck bowed against his will into a posture of servility.

He wrenched at the muscles until they threatened to

cut off his breath from the pressure, but he could move his head no higher than it was.

Then, while Valonicus chuckled somewhere behind him in the howling snow, Brak's knees jerked him forward. Against his will he found himself crawling forward until he was staring down at Garr's boots. Slowly his arms bent and his head came down until his forehead barely touched the toes. He straightened, only to bend forward again.

Inside Brak's mind a red mist congealed, but it was a rage without outlet. He tried to hurl a curse at the wizard, but no sound came from his lips. He struggled to break the force of the spell by holding his body motionless, but that was as futile as trying to force movement on it. He could hear Garr laughing, and somewhere Nari was sobbing like a madwoman.

Brak strained his thews until pain screamed through his body, but he could not break the invisible vise of power that held him in a doglike posture at Garr's feet. The laughter of the would-be prince went on rising until it subsided into a series of uncontrolled hiccoughs, as if the sight of Brak was becoming too hilarious to bear.

"Very well," Garr finally gasped. "Enough, Valonicus!"

"Shall I release him for execution or leave him as he is, sire?" Valonicus asked.

"How long will your spell last?"

"Perhaps long enough for him to freeze to death in the snow. Or perhaps a little less. It should be amusing to have the poor fool spend his last minutes wondering whether he'll be able to move his body before the storm buries him. By the time it wears off, in any event, he'll be in no condition to trouble us."

"Then leave him as he is, by all means," Garr decided. He chuckled. "He'll make a pretty statue for travelers in the spring to wonder at."

Raising his voice, the Lord Garr began ordering his two remaining soldiers to resume their journey. One of them hastily disposed of his dead comrade while the other tied Nari onto the back of a horse.

Brak's mind tried to move his eyes, but he had to depend on his ears for what happened next. He heard the accouterments of animals jingling as they moved through the snow. Nari moaned as she was lifted onto the horse. Then he heard Valonicus observe that it would be prudent to strip the girl and bring forth the rest of the map by the only means left them as soon as they could find a convenient shelter.

Garr's laughter was the last sound Brak heard before they rode off. The man was obviously pleased and sure that he'd have the lost treasure by nightfall and the throne of Gilgamarch before the spring thaws.

Frozen on hands and knees, Brak felt the snow covering him.

7

Presently Brak heard the wind change direction and begin to die down. The snowfall diminished slowly to a trickle of flakes as the storm must be moving eastward and away. Barely within his view he could see that the rugged walls of the Mountains of Smoke were standing forth again, except for clouds that hovered over the highest peaks in the east. A wan and chilly light poured down from the sun.

Immobilized in the position in which the spell had left him, Brak was barely able to blink his eyelids and knock the rime of frost from them. The distant pass was clearly visible now, as was the skull-like formation of ebony rock.

The big barbarian's mind seemed to be functioning well enough, but there was now no sensation in his body. He noticed the low angle of the sun from his own shadow cast on the snow. There was no more than an hour or two of daylight left. If his body wasn't already freezing with cold, the night would surely finish him.

Once more he strained his body, concentrating all his mind on the single task of lifting his right hand from the snow that buried it to well above the wrist.

Nothing moved. It was as though unyielding, invisible iron encased him.

He tried again, groaning inwardly, straining and writhing with the effort he exerted to stir the slightest bit of motion out of his numbed hand. There was no response, though now he could feel the pain of his efforts more strongly.

Rage rose in his mind, until the world turned red in front of him. It spread through him, bringing a flood of pain that only increased the mounting anger. He'd never die until he could see Garr and Valonicus dying like curs at his feet!

He cursed himself and tried to raise his fist toward his foes in the ancient gesture of habit.

Abruptly he felt the knuckles of the hand bend. Within the snow he could now feel that the flattened fingers had curled and lifted from the frozen ground. But a second effort to make a fist yielded no results.

His mind was still seething with fury, but it was a cold rage now, refined beyond any anger he had ever felt. He could feel the strength gathering in him, and he conserved it, thinking of how that hidden hand would look if he curled his fingers against his palm. And finally, when every detail of the motion was clear in his mind, he released his strength in a burst.

For a moment he seemed to be succeeding. Then the effort was spent, and his hand lay flat upon the ground again.

He groaned in frustration—and the sound was suddenly loud in his ears. It was the first cry to pass between his lips since the incantation of Valonicus had wrenched him into this craven pose.

Again he gathered his strength and willed his fingers to bend, *bend*. His teeth ground together, and his whole body ached with the strain. A piercing pain struck between his eyes, almost blackening out his mind.

And the fingers bent slowly, slowly . . .

They touched his frozen palm, and his hand was a fist.

Harsh laughter broke from his lips, and this time the fist raised slightly—raised and shook!

The pain between his eyes grew stronger, but he refused to give in to it now. If pain was the price of movement, then every bit of pain was precious!

It took long minutes before he could force his arm to throw him sideways from his kneeling position. It took longer and gave him more trouble before he could straighten his legs and his back. The pain increased, forcing him to stop and rest between efforts. But every time the pain stopped him, he called back to his mind the laughter of Lord Garr, the yellow eyes of Valonicus, and the moan of the girl as her abductors carried her away. Bit by bit he brought his body under control.

His shadow was long on the snow when he stood upright.

He had expected to find his hands frozen from the long exposure to the cold of the ground. But now as he moved about carefully, he felt none of the numbness he had feared. His fingers tingled slightly, but that was a good sign. Maybe the rage he felt had kept his circulation going strongly enough to save them. Or maybe the spell of Valonicus was partly potent against even such changes as the freezing of his flesh.

He rubbed the aching muscles of his neck and stared at the pass toward which they had gone and the skull-rock that marked the way toward their goal. He had to choose one as his path.

Prudence dictated a speedy march to the pass. But prudence had lost the battle long before, while he lay trapped in the spell and fighting to make a fist of defiance. He was worried about Nari, but there was more at stake than merely saving a strange girl with a living treasure map on her back.

No man from the high steppes and wild lands of the north could be made to grovel without someone paying dearly!

His body was still shaky and hard to control, but he could move fairly well now. He began searching the snow for his broadsword. At length he found it at the bottom of a drift, and a howl of satisfaction came from his lips.

With the lion tail and the savage yellow braid of hair swinging free behind him, he began to climb through the knee-deep drifts, humming a tuneless melody from the hate songs of his ancestors. His face was set toward the target of the skull-rock perhaps two leagues distant, and he increased his speed toward it as the last of the spell wore away.

Valonicus had said that the big barbarian might endure the spell to its ending with some life in him, but hardly that Brak would have enough vitality to give chase. But then the wizard had cast no spells to test the weather and had not expected the abrupt change, though such changes seemed to plague these forlorn peaks at the eastern edge of the world.

Little additional snow had fallen after they left Brak behind, and he had no difficulty in following the tracks of the riders and their dozen pack animals.

He worked his way steadily upward, departing from the trail in order to survey its next bending from a convenient crag. The day was ending, and the light was already waning. The sky had turned a cold, deep blue. Now the first stars emerged.

Brak began to worry about losing the trail in the

dark. The wind still shifted the snow about, making constant observation necessary to spot the marks the animals had made. With the coming of night he would have to move a step at a time, stopping to peer closely for the signs. They could easily escape him then if the wind kept playing with the tracks or if more snow began to fall.

Then Brak stood up, and a wolfish grin came to his lips. He wasn't far behind, after all. The wind had carried a sound to his ears that could only be the voice of one of Garr's soldiers. Then other sounds came, indicating that both men were shouting angrily at themselves or at their animals.

Brak's wonder at what difficulty they were having was soon answered as he edged forward to the lip of an icy promontory. With the wind flattening his cheeks, he studied the gorge below.

In the deep shadows down there he could make out the two men wrestling with the train of pack animals. The second pair of beasts had become stuck in a small landslip, leaving all but the lead pair to mill about aimlessly behind them, jerking on their tethers but unable to pass on. Most of the packs had already been stripped, and the men were trying to transfer the burdens from the last animals past the struggling pair that had been trapped. Obviously they were using the free lead animals to carry everything ahead before they began the difficult task of disposing of those trapped and leading the others around the rubble that had fallen across the trail.

That meant that the Lord Garr and Valonicus must have gone on to find a campsite for the night.

High above the struggle Brak wondered how he could slip past the gorge, outrun the soldiers, and come upon the two he wanted while they were unguarded. He leaned far over, studying the path. Then, as he pulled back, his elbow struck an icy rock. It spiraled down into the gorge and clattered against the side of the cliff below.

8

The men below raised their heads, and one threw up a hand to point to the barbarian. Brak was sliding backward as the other soldier nocked an arrow to his bow and sent it whistling.

The arrow missed as Brak ducked. But in his haste to escape it, he threw his body too far to the side. His foot skidded on the icy surface, and his left side slipped off the promontory's edge. He could feel himself slipping over, and fear thickened in him as he fought for balance.

He flung out his hands to catch the edge as he fell, and his fingertips slipped painfully on the ice-covered rock. Now he needed every vestige of strength in his great hands as he squeezed down, trying to find a firmer grip. Somehow he held on, dangling in the air with his broadsword slapping against his thigh.

The soldiers were howling in glee. Both had arrows nocked, and in another moment the big barbarian's body would be pierced through by at least one of them. He struggled futilely to pull himself upward—

There was a sudden creaking sound from the promontory, and he felt something vibrate. Turning his head carefully, he could make out a fissure that was beginning to appear across the middle above him. In a few seconds the whole ledge was going to break off and crash down into the gorge.

As he turned his eyes back, he saw one arrow flashing toward him. The arrow dug a channel of blood through his right calf. And the other soldier was getting set for another shot.

No chance was good, but his eyes and mind had been busy hunting for the least certain way to death. Now he began to sway, exerting all his strength, kicking and hauling his free swinging legs back and forth until his body was a pendulum. An arrow hissed through the air to one side of his head. He cursed and swung harder. The fissure widened and cracked.

A split second before the promontory broke, Brak let go. He plunged downward and a little sideways, to where a tiny ledge offered a grip for his hands. He couldn't hang onto it, but it slowed his fall and let him swing to the side again, where there was a rough area that he could use to brake his downward plunge. Finally he struck with jarring force into a deep snowbank.

The promontory tumbled past him, falling end over end like a juggernaut. One of the soldiers screamed, but the other watched silently, with an open mouth. It struck, raising clouds of snow. The pack animals went mad, biting their trace lines, stamping, kicking, and rearing.

Brak clambered from the snow, shaking his head to clear it of dizziness. His hands were sore with a hundred scratches, and blood leaked from his bare leg to leave a trail on the white crust of snow as he skidded and stumbled to the bottom of the gorge.

He pulled his broadsword, giving his first attention to the animals. He slashed the traces of those still alive and cut the lines between each pair. Freed, they bolted up the trail.

For a long moment Brak stared down by the ruin left by the fallen promontory. Two men and two ani-

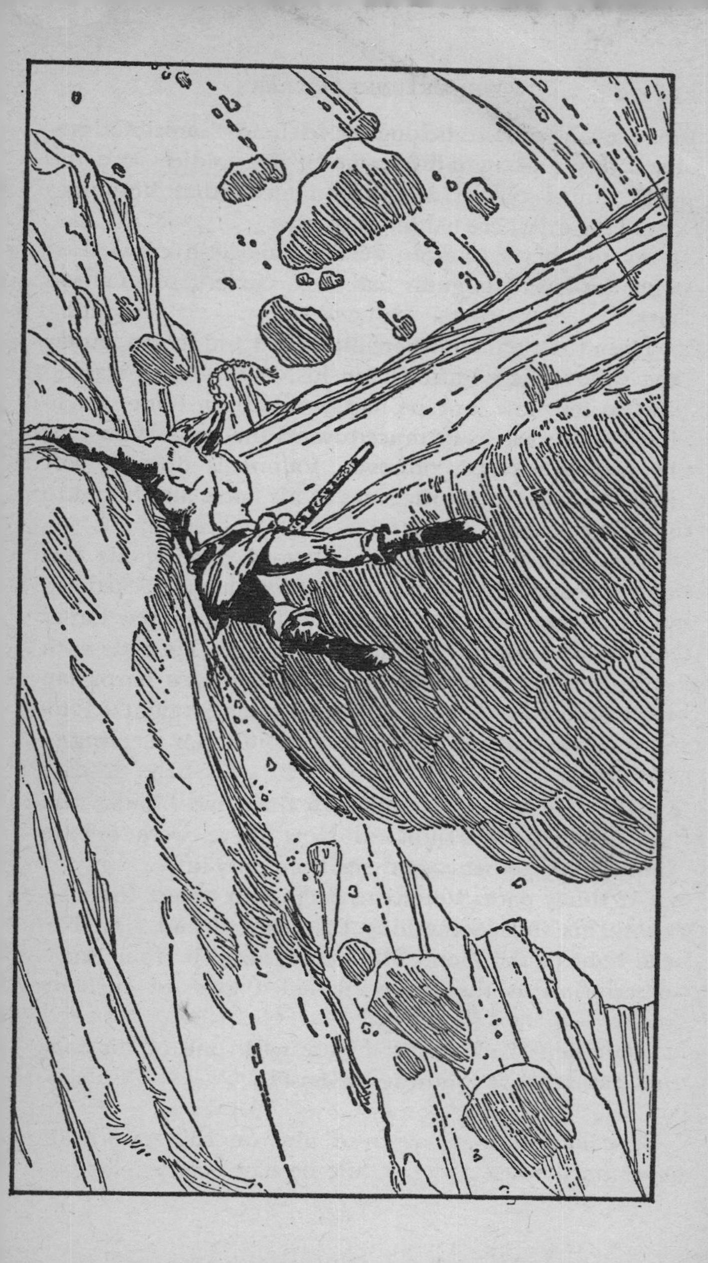

that, the wizard could have ridden by unnoticed, perhaps to see what had become of the soldiers and the pack animals. And that would mean that Valonicus could be anywhere behind him now.

As the big barbarian turned, his flesh crawled at what he saw. His guess had been correct, but far too late.

Near the boulder where Brak had hidden to survey the valley, the wizard sat on his horse. There was no way to tell how long he had been sitting there watching Brak's stealthy advance toward the tents. Now that he was discovered, however, Valonicus dug his soft tooled boots against the sides of his horse and began to canter forward.

Brak yanked out his broadsword, licking his lips that were suddenly dry. Valonicus' horse kicked up puffs of snow, and the wizard's yellow eyes grew larger and more compelling as he drew nearer. He rode with no sign of a weapon in his hand, against a barbarian with his sword at ready. Yet he came straight on toward Brak, neither rushing too rapidly nor seeming to hesitate.

The yellow eyes flashed with their evil humor, and the bony mouth smirked. Now there were only a hundred paces between them, then only fifty.

At thirty paces Valonicus pulled an object from beneath his robe—something that flashed and glared in the light of the moon. Brak recognized it from Nari's description as the cheap two-sided glass of enchantment.

Valonicus flicked the mirror with one of his long nails and sent it spinning furiously.

9

Still twenty paces away Valonicus reined in, still holding the spinning mirror before him. Brak heard the deep whistling sound he remembered with horror from the cave.

Try as he would, the barbarian seemed unable to stare anywhere but into the blurring disc of the mirror. For fragmented seconds he saw his own image reflected in it, and the hair on the nape of his neck rose.

"So you followed us after all," Valonicus called. His voice seemed to echo from an immense distance. "Outlanders are sometimes noted for their stamina, but not for their wits. Well, you'll go no further."

"Get down and fight!" Brak challenged him. "Stand down like a man!"

"Nonsense," Valonicus replied. "I never fight when others will do it for me. Others, such as barbarians!"

His voice rose to a taunt on the last words. The mirror spun and spun, forming a blinding bar of silver light across Brak's vision.

With a low growl Brak charged at the wizard.

He had taken only three steps when a radiant gray cloud materialized before him. He choked with horror as the cloud took on shape and coalesced into a shambling, transparent figure with a huge sword clutched in its hand.

Brak reeled back. He recognized the planes of the phantom's face and the long yellow braid that was swinging down behind the phantom's cloak. There was even the familiar tuft of the lion tail dangling below the hide garment the phantom seemed to wear.

Brak knew that this phantom was himself.

The mirror spun, and a second cloud sprang up. A second ghostly Brak appeared, with stars glimmering through his transparent skull.

Valonicus' finger sent the disc spinning faster, and there was another phantom. Then a fourth appeared. The mouths of the apparitions opened on savage clenched teeth.

In his travels Brak had thought he had faced almost every possible opponent. But he had never been forced to battle against himself.

Now there were a score of the cloudy things, each with his own appearance, each mimicking his advances. Valonicus had nearly disappeared behind the line of marching ghosts. Only his yellow eyes and the silvery flare of the revolving mirror could be seen.

Brak took a tighter grip on his broadsword and charged into the line of shadow-creatures, praying to the nameless gods of his youth. He hacked out wildly, bent on slaughter.

But his judgment had failed him again, as his first touch of broadsword to apparition proved. The terrible force emanating from the phantoms jolted him, lifting him and flinging him a great distance, to crash down in the snow with an uncontrollable yell of pain.

His sword was useless against the creatures of the demon glass. It was worse than useless—it was a weapon for their use.

Now the specters changed direction, shambling toward the big barbarian as he clawed out of the snow heap and faced them with the futile sword dangling from his numbed hand. The apparitions came on steadily, forcing Brak to back away. There was no way to strike against them. And once they gripped him with the massed force of the emanations, he would almost certainly be torn apart and flung in pieces across the whole snowy vastness of the valley.

While the keening, whistling sound of the mirror grew louder, the phantoms advanced steadily, forcing Brak to retreat reluctant step by step.

With the only faint hope he had, Brak began to work his way left. The phantoms kept coming, floating a hand's width above the snowy crust and ever nearer. He knew he was close to death, and somehow the knowledge steadied him.

From the corner of his eye the barbarian saw that Valonicus still sat his horse in the same spot where he had begun his attack. Brak continued his steady retreat, but now he let little moaning sounds slip from his mouth, loud enough for Valonicus to hear and enjoy over the keening of the mirror. Summoning an imitation of terror wasn't hard. He literally had to fight himself to keep from screaming at the sight of the ghastly phalanx of transparent images of himself marching steadily closer.

Suddenly he heard the jingle of the harness on Valonicus' horse. The wizard had either sensed the tactic or grown anxious for a different view. He had the reins in his hands now, prepared to ride out of range.

Brak spun around. With the knowledge of the nearness of the apparitions driving him toward panic, the big barbarian called on the skills he had learned as a youth in the high steppes. He slid his palm around on the hilt of the big broadsword and flung the massive weapon like a lance.

The wizard cursed and reared his horse. His yellow eyes were burning like bonfires as the broadsword tumbled toward him, making a slow end-over-end motion through the air as it shot upward. Valonicus' mount leaped forward, but too late. The tumbling sword struck the mirror and shattered it in the wizard's hand.

The apparitions exploded in puffs of sound and smoke.

Valonicus shrieked. His eyes turned bright red, and from the hand that had held the mirror a column of flame spurted skyward. There was a hissing and the screaming voice of Valonicus as the wizard's hand began to char and melt away, going up in steam and dripping onto the snow. Where the droplets fell, the crust sent up little clouds of hot vapor.

The stallion was bucking wildly, but the wizard stayed in the saddle somehow, and the unburned hand groped into a pouch at his side, his reddened eyes blazing toward Brak. The sorcerer should have been dead.

Brak had charged after his sword. Now he scooped it up in both hands, raising it high as he charged. His leap carried him high above the ground, and the sword began arcing downward just as Valonicus withdrew a long-nailed hand from the pouch.

The big broadsword went through the wizard's skull with almost no resistance, carrying downward to cleave into a shoulder and out as Brak's leap carried him to the left.

A single horrible cry wailed upward toward the sky, seeming to lose itself among the stars. Then the stallion was plunging forward madly, with the corpse of Valonicus still clinging to the saddle. The horse plunged toward the fur pavilion just as the Lord Garr was emerging.

Garr held a dagger in his hand, and he was dragging

Nari with him. The girl was naked from the waist upward. Neither was looking toward the scene of Brak's victory.

Valonicus' horse thundered straight toward the fire-lit pavilion with the wizard still in the saddle. The burned stump of an arm flapped loosely at his side, and the horse charged on, unheeding of what lay ahead.

Lord Garr and Nari were directly in the path of the beast when the usurper prince finally looked up. He cried out and thrust Nari aside as Valonicus came roaring past, and the wild hooves of the animal just missed him as the horse ripped through the fur pavilion, scattering coals of fire.

The dead wizard and the fear-crazed mount raced on toward the crevasse that lay just a short distance beyond the tents. They reached the edge of the chasm with no slackening of speed. Briefly, like a macabre dancer, the horse pawed the emptiness beneath him. Then with a piercing animal scream of terror, they disappeared.

For many moments the scream echoed and reechoed to show the depth of the crevasse. Then it was stilled.

10

Something flickered brightly, and Brak turned to see Nari struggling with Garr. The light from the overturned fire glinted from a dagger in her hand which she must have seized from him when his attention was diverted by the horse. Brak cried out and began running toward the fight.

But it was over before he could reach them. Nari had the dagger above her head, bringing it down awkwardly. Lord Garr's head was back and he was off-balance. He threw up an arm to ward off the blow. Nari rammed the dagger into his throat and twisted it ferociously.

Blood poured from Garr's mouth. He took three staggering steps and smashed face downward into the snow.

Weak and numbed by the wound in his leg, Brak stumbled toward the corpse that had been Lord Garr. Nari was bent over it, pulling the dagger free of the dead man's neck. Brak had a quick glimpse of her back. It was now completely covered from the base of the neck to the base of the spine with the strange markings. On this living map he recognized the valley and the crevasse that were overlooked by the skull-rock.

Then he got a better look and swore in sick disgust. The map was complete—but the lower half of her back was covered with raw blisters. He could guess the reason for the fire in the pavilion now!

Nari faced him with the knife dripping in her hand. If she felt pain, she gave no sign of it.

"Lord Garr found the map," she told him. "He got it without the potion, as Valonicus told him he could. He did it by himself, and he liked doing it!"

"I saw." Brak had trouble standing, and his legs were growing more wobbly by the minute. "Well, now the treasure belongs to you and no one else. The rest of them are all dead. Come on, girl. There may be something in the wizard's tent to heal you."

Nari gave a strange laugh. "Nothing can heal me. The Lord Garr used me ill in his tent. He beat me and mocked me. He told me what I really meant to him. And he laid hands on my body—"

She began to shudder. And suddenly Brak became aware of an odd singsong note in her voice, like that of a child crooning to a doll.

"The treasure of Tobool was left to me by my father," she crooned. "And now it is mine. Lord Garr wants to take it away from me, but he can't have it. He's a man. He's greedy—"

Brak frowned at her, slowly realizing that the ruin of her life's dream, the nightmare experiences of the last few days, and finally the tortures of this night had driven her to a kind of madness. He sighed wearily, wondering how he could cope with her and get her to let him treat her back. As he was thinking, Nari attacked him. His response was uncertain and his leg moved stiffly as he tried to evade her. He skidded as the dagger flashed for his face. He wrenched his head aside, but the knife point raked the bridge of his nose. If he had been a trifle slower, it would have torn out his eye.

She began backing away, more rapidly than he could keep up with her. Smoke was gusting into his face, and he saw that the fur pavilion of Lord Garr had started to burn, probably from one of the wind blown coals. Nari backed through it with no sign that she could feel the heat.

Brak had to detour around the fire, and she was further from him when he saw her again. She was still backing away from him. He called softly, trying to make his voice soothing to her. "Don't go that way, girl. All I want is to make you feel better. You're sick."

"Yes," she agreed. She nodded sagely with a little girl's wisdom. "Sick. All men are sick. Greedy and nasty and sick."

"Nari, stop!"

His cry was useless. She gave another backward skip away from him. Retreating, she overstepped the lip of the crevasse. Her scream was a long time dying.

Dawn broke clear and piercingly cold. Brak had already risen and bundled himself in extra cloaks from the pavilion of Valonicus. He ate from rations he found there and helped himself to a small pouch of coins. Then he tramped back across the valley floor in search of his broadsword and Lord Garr's stallion.

The horse had broken its picket rope during the height of the confusion the preceding night, but it came when he called and whinnied when he stroked its head.

Sleep and food had refreshed him, and his wound was closed now. But an immense weariness filled the big barbarian as he rode the stallion to the lip of the crevasse. This morning, with the sun glaring behind the Mountains of Smoke, it was possible to see down into the vast chasm.

On a floor of ice which spread across the crevasse far below he made out the remains of Valonicus' horse. Nearby lay the body of the wizard. Ironically Nari had fallen quite near the sorcerer. One outflung hand rested across his mouth as if she was caressing his face in death.

Most of the ice was rough and covered with snow. But where the horse had landed, a great ledge of it had been splintered off. There the ice was clear—so clear that Brak could plainly see the dazzle of metal ingots of gold and the jeweled spillage of carved chests.

Brak was the only living man who even knew such a treasure existed now.

He would leave it to its dead.

The black skull-rock guarding the valley seemed to frown at him. He shuddered and drew his warm cloak up tight around his neck, making the bag of coins jingle against his broadsword. Gently he urged the stallion away from the lip of the precipice.

Brak said Nari's name once aloud. Then he rode onward across the shining ice and the cloud-blown pass to freedom.